BRAIDED LIES

A Thousand Islands Castle Mystery

*To Christy —
Enjoy this gem
of a mystery.
Catherine D'Agostino*

Catherine D'Agostino

This is a work of fiction. Characters, organizations, events and descriptions are the product of the author's imagination. Any resemblance to actual people, living or dead, is entirely coincidental.

First published in the United States by Iron Pelican Publications, LLC. ™

Braided Lies: A Thousand Islands Castle Mystery.
Copyright © 2023 by Catherine D'Agostino

All rights reserved. No part of this book may be reproduced in any form without permission from the author or publisher, except as permitted by U.S. copyright law.

www.ironpelicanpublications.com

Cover design by Catherine D'Agostino

ISBN 979-8-9880009-2-1

First edition: 2023

I'm indebted to early readers of this story, including Mom, Ginnie, Margaret, Megan, Ron, Michael, Beth, Claudia and Susan. Their encouragement, recommendations and attention to detail were second to none. And special thanks to Lake Shore Center for the Arts in Westfield, NY, for its commitment to nurturing and promoting good storytelling.

To Jack, of course.

To Carter and Brooke,
who asked for short chapters.

"Love goes by in haps;
Some Cupid kills with arrows,
some with traps."

-- *William Shakespeare, Much Ado About Nothing*

PROLOGUE

June 20, 1990

Brian Annetti and Patty Flanagan paddled their oars hard to reach the island's shore before nightfall. Graduation rehearsal started at ten the following day in the Alexandria Bay High School Auditorium. They ignored the pouring rain. On Brian's count to three, the two pulled the red canoe onto the grass under the swaying arms of a willow.

The two intruders crept across the castle's front lawn and then sprinted down a stone walkway, slipping behind an orange construction sign that warned them to *Keep Out*. Brian's dark curls, t-shirt and shorts were soaked. He checked to see if the security cameras above the stone parapet were pointed in his direction. Whiffs of coconut from Patty's skin, remnants of her day at the beach with friends, itched at his nose. He rubbed his eyes to hide his attempt for another view of her tight cropped top. He watched drops of water drip from her blond ponytail.

He was intense. She chewed gum.

Patty turned to her accomplice. "You're sure there is a treasure in there?"

Brian craned his neck up at the castle that loomed over them. He pointed to an iron trellis that ran to a third-story window. "The only way to get into the library is to climb the trellis and go in that window." His voice quivered with false bravado.

Patty stood, crossing her arms across her chest. "No way I am doing that."

"You want the diamonds or not?"

"Ugh." Patty crouched back down and slid off her flip-flops. "Take these. I don't want to slip."

Brian shook his head. "Put them in the backpack."

"I left it in the canoe," Patty said.

Brian let out a low groan. *Damn it,* he thought. "I thought you grabbed it."

"I just slid some sticks of gum and the matchbook into my back pocket. Want me to go back for it?"

"Forget it. I don't want to take any chances of being seen. Let's go."

Moments later, Brian was ahead of Patty climbing the sturdy lattice in their summer concert garb, he in his Pearl Jam t-shirt and she in her REM midriff tank. They trudged up and into the building.

In the blackened room, the seniors waited with their backs straight against the wall. Being townies, they knew the revolving flash from the Sunken Rock Lighthouse would give them light every forty-five seconds. When the beam cut the darkness, they inhaled their gasps as bright prisms reflected off long-forgotten items. The room, with its floor-to-ceiling bookshelves, crippled piano, and cobweb-laced candelabra, would have impressed Poe himself.

The high school seniors didn't move when the light left the window, plunging them back into darkness.

"I thought I saw candles on the piano," Patty said, fumbling in her pocket for the matchbook. She pulled it out, never seeing an empty silver gum wrapper flit down to the floor.

She tried to step forward, but Brian held her back. "Wait for one more flash before we move."

He got his wish.

And when the light returned, their gaze locked onto an enormous oil painting of the couple responsible for the castle's name, Griffin and Faith Quill. The commissioned piece was secured to the plastered wall between two tall windows whose curtains were a velvety plum. Griffin Quill wore a black military uniform with brass pins and colorful medals decorating his lapel. A bulky man, his closely trimmed gray mustache and beard made him appear distinguished as he stood beside his young wife. In her full-length, corseted navy-blue dress, Faith Quill was all curves to her husband's sharp angles. She chose white accents – silk gloves, ivory pearls, flowerpot hat, milliner feathers – that made her look even more youthful than matronly.

Darkness returned.

"He looked mean," Patty said.

Brian seized the opportunity to impress. "My great-grandfather once transported Quill and his buddies to the train station during a winter storm. He said Vanderbilt and Carnegie tipped him a hundred bucks. Each."

Patty was not listening. With a flick of her wrist, she struck a match and stepped forward to light the low candles. She turned to Brian. "Take me to the jewels."

Brian lifted his shirt and pulled out a crushed roll of papers from the elastic waistband of his shorts. He unrolled the white pages, smoothing them out in the steady light. "My dad's days as construction foreman would be over if he knew I borrowed these. He would kill me."

Patty stepped toward the oil painting, unknowingly kicking the gum wrapper under the door and into the unseen hall. She ran her hand across its thick, golden frame. "Ah, the Gilded Age." She looked up to God. "Thank you, AP History."

Brian's thoughts returned to the backpack in the canoe and then to Patty's halter top.

"Look here," he said, tapping the blueprints. "See this unlabeled area on the second floor? My dad said he found a hidden staircase to the kitchen after the crew knocked down a wall last week. No one knew it was there, not even the architects."

Patty frowned. "So, you don't know *for sure* that there is treasure here?"

Brian assured her. "The area with the secret stairs has thicker lines than all the others. Look here," he said, pointing at the plans.

"This space behind the library has those same lines. There is a secret room behind these bookshelves."

Patty sidled up to him for a closer look. Brian felt her warm breath on his neck.

Eager now, he rolled up the plans and tucked them inside his waistband. "There must be a handle or knob around here to open this wall." He moved the candles closer, then ran his fingertips under a shelf of dusty books.

Patty followed suit, searching along the wooden board below his.

The lighthouse nestled in the St. Lawrence River completed a few more revolutions before Patty gasped. "Oh! I feel something in this corner."

"What is it?" Brian held his breath.

"Some sort of metal thingy."

"Pull it."

Patty obeyed. A soft click made the wall of books wobble. "We found it," she squealed.

Sounds of distant shouting halted her celebration.

A woman's voice howled first. "Let go of me!"

A man's voice replied. "No one can hear you."

Patty hissed at Brian. "You said no one was here."

"Then we have to hurry." Brian set his palms on the shelves. "Help me push."

The rusty hinges creaked open, releasing odors of musty stillness. In the dim candlelight, they saw an unfinished bedroom chamber. Quickly, the teens moved their eyes over the room's landscape – a high-back chair facing a tall window, a stack of quilts and pillows, a makeshift dressing table constructed of wooden crates. On the tabletop sat a tray of sparkling gems.

"Pearls," Brian whispered.

Patty cracked her gum. "Rubies."

Without an ounce of care, the teens lunged toward the jewels.

After taking only a few steps forward, the century-old floorboards cracked and collapsed, stopping their forward progression, and sending their bodies falling down an abandoned shaft. Their screams echoed for far too long, ending sharply with two solid thuds, one after the other. There was no call for help, no moan of pain, no way for the high school seniors to go back in time, to climb back into the red canoe, to push it into the river, to return home for the long-planned graduation ceremonies and celebrations that awaited them the following day.

From high above, a dark figure flashed light down onto the two broken, lifeless bodies entwined in a clumsy embrace. A full minute passed. A decision was made. The grainy sound of shuffling feet retreating from the jagged hole was replaced by a soft click as the pivoting door was pulled closed by bloodied hands.

PART ONE

A few days shy of
twenty-five years later

CHAPTER 1

Ash Burton stood on the sidewalk outside *The River Gazette* pointing his index finger into the editor's face.

"My, oh my. Would you look at that?" He had never seen a port-wine birthmark up close before. "Hereditary, maybe," he mumbled to himself.

Opal Schatz narrowed her eyes. At sixty-three years old, she certainly *should* have been used to her facial splotch attracting sharp glances, low gasps, and (not so soft) whispers. But she could never adjust to the wagging finger, the feeling of being treated like she was an artifact on public display in some Freak Museum. She knew full well that it wasn't the fourth day of an unrelenting heat wave that released the sweat dripping down her back, moistening her white linen jumper. No. It was this man's direct rudeness that churned humiliation in her gut.

"Perhaps a magnifying glass would help," Opal said to her scheduled interview and his extended arm. She had expected him to respond as others had responded over her last six-plus decades of life

– to drop his arm and offer profuse apologies. While the former action happened, to Opal's surprise, the latter did not. She watched Ash Burton's eyes trace her scarlet patch's perimeter from brow to nose to ear.

"Mr. Burton," she said firmly. "Thank you for agreeing to this interview about the DNA results on such a nice day." She stepped back to let him shuffle by her and into the newspaper lobby. Standing on the sidewalk a moment longer, she reminded herself of the reason she had requested the interview.

You need his confirmation. Don't be a snit.

Ash sat across from Opal, setting a notebook and pen on the conference table in her office. When he removed his plaid ivy cap and straightened his thinning snow-white hair, Opal could not help but run her hand through her own grays, which she knew now outnumbered her auburn strands ten to one. She had expected the architect to be more distinguished, not a tweed-suited gnome with two black nose hairs peeking out of his right nostril.

Opal slid a manilla folder under her legal pad; she had a copy of the DNA reports ready if he asked her to review them. She tapped the long yellow pages with the tip of her pen, knowing precisely which questions to ask and in what order to ask them. When she looked up to thank him again for agreeing to the interview, she saw that her guest was not listening. His eyes were focused over her shoulder and out the large picture window that took up most of her office's back wall.

Opal swiveled her chair and saw the reason for his distraction. She followed his stare to find that his eyes were firmly planted on the magnificent structure rising out of a speck of land on the St. Lawrence River, just a quarter mile offshore. There she stood in all her glory – Quill Castle – with her copper turrets proudly standing high and majestic against the blue sky. It was as though Jack's magic seeds had gone wild, producing a six-story Rhineland castle instead of a beanstalk.

Opal and Ash could not turn away from the romance, the aura, of her existence. In their shared silence, they watched a two-story ferry boat arrive at her dock as another pulled away. Still another vessel, jampacked with paying customers and amateur photographers, was halfway through a complete revolution around the island, fulfilling its promise of providing unobstructed views from every angle. Like a hypnotist releasing a patient, Opal snapped back to the reality of her office and cleared her throat.

"It is an honor to finally meet the region's expert on the Quill family," she said, redirecting her guest's attention to the task at hand. "You have been on my contacts list for quite some time."

He returned the accolades. "I've read your articles. All of them," he said. "I used to design bridges by day and study local history by night. Since retiring, I have more time to delve into the Quill family's background and research some uncharted areas."

"Like what?" Opal asked.

Ash's face flushed with enthusiasm. "I've recently learned that designers of Gilded Age castles often planned secret chambers without marking them on blueprints."

Opal tilted her head. "I didn't know that."

Ash smiled broadly. "I found one off the Singer Castle library and wouldn't be surprised if I found the same thing out there," he said, winking while pointing at Quill Castle through the window.

After making a mental note of his suggestion, Opal clicked the end of her pen. "Let's get started, shall we?"

Opal had every intention of launching her first question until Ash Burton interrupted.

"Everyone knows the names and works of Andrew Carnegie and J.D. Rockefeller, but few know the accomplishments of Griffin Quill," Ash said. "He never made the history books. Do you know why, Mrs. Schatz?"

Opal shook her head, sensing a sudden shift in *her* interview.

"Griffin Quill was the go-to man behind the scenes, the one who became rich and famous by pampering the rich and famous. His Braybury Hotel was New York City's jewel from the day of its first opening. You should see the pictures," Ash said, his voice giddy. "Most expected Quill to be an overbearing yes-man, but he had the one trait that propelled him into the world of luxury. Do you know what that trait was, Mrs. Schatz?"

Opal sat back in her chair, tossing her pen onto the yellow paper.

Ash answered his own question.

"Charm. That's what it was. He had charm. People liked him. He transformed the hotel industry as we know it." Ash could not hide his enthusiasm and awe. "He is the one who created room service. The web of his influence extends far and wide. No wonder he and Faith were so in love that she never knew the meaning of the word 'want.'

If I have said it once, I have said it a thousand times, they were the first modern American love story." Ash pounded his fist on the table. "And you can quote me on that."

Ash Burton's comment rang familiar to Opal. "I first learned about their lives decades ago when I read the script to tourists on *The Rhineland* ferry," she said. "My friends, Mac and Ellie McAllister, own the fleet. I remember reading that phrase into a microphone, that Griffin and Faith Quill were the first modern American love story."

Ash leaned forward. His eyes gleamed. "That's because I wrote that script."

I give up, Opal thought.

He plowed ahead. "When the first phase of the castle's restoration ended in the 1980s, Alexandria Bay did not have the resources or staffing to accommodate the wave of tourists that descended on us. Fortunately, local leaders seized an opportunity and committed to figuring out how to market history."

Opal sighed. Ash continued.

"That is when I came into the picture. They needed a historian to help them turn this area into the multi-million-dollar industry it is today, and I was the closest thing to a historian as they could find."

"Thank you for sharing that with me, Mr. Burton, but I must insist on continuing the interview."

"Of course," he said. "How old are you?"

"What?" Opal said.

He laughed to himself. "I know it is the one question women don't like to be asked, but if you could just bear with me. How old are you?" he repeated, clicking his pen, ready to jot down her answer.

"Sixty-three."

"And your husband's name?"

"Daniel."

"Alive or deceased?"

"Deceased," Opal said, her voice cracking on the first syllable.

Ash's expression softened. "When?"

Opal cleared her throat. "Last year, 2014."

"Does Ruby have any children?" Ash said.

She cocked her head. "How do you know my daughter's name is Ruby?"

Ash Burton looked up at her. "I'm here investigating the birthstone branch of the Quill family. Griffin and Faith's third child, Pearl, had a daughter named Jade who had a daughter named Opal who had a daughter named Ruby. Are you not the Opal in that family line?"

"I ... I am," she stuttered.

"So, you are the great-granddaughter of Griffin and Faith Quill."

"Mr. Burton. That was what I had always believed."

Ash's warm smile faded on her next words.

"Until last week."

CHAPTER 2

Opal had no doubt she saw a flicker of concern flash across Ash Burton's face, so she seized the opportunity to begin the interview she had intended to conduct.

"It's no secret that a vast majority of Alex-Bayers wholeheartedly believe that they are blood descendants of the Quill family in some way, shape or form," Opal began. "The newspaper decided to find out if this were true."

Ash nodded. Opal continued.

"About six months ago, the newspaper sponsored advanced DNA testing for anyone who wanted to confirm the legitimacy of their family lines. I included myself in the sampling, and, along with my sister-in-law, Claudine Schatz, and about forty others from town, we submitted our swabs to an ancestry company. We received the results last week." Opal slid the folder out from under her legal pad and pushed it toward him across the table.

Ash reached into his jacket pocket for a pair of reading glasses and set them on the bridge of his nose. He opened the folder and began reading charts, graphs and summaries of data.

Opal watched him read. With each passing page, his vibrant demeanor faded, his shoulders slumped. After he turned the last page, he removed his glasses and tucked them back into his pocket.

"This data is incorrect. These findings are simply not possible."

When Opal tried to interrupt, he held up his hand signaling her to stop. "Let me be clear: Griffin and Faith Quill had three children – Griffin, Jr., Cecelia, and Pearl. This is common knowledge."

Opal spoke softly. "Mr. Burton. The report clearly shows that I am the descendent of Faith Quill, but not of Griffin Quill. A large chunk of my hereditary line is missing."

Ash shook his head. "Not possible."

Opal let his words hang in the air before resuming. "In my recent research, I found a few references that suggest Faith may have had an affair with a member of the staff, perhaps an overseas worker from Germany."

Ash frowned, sliding the reports back to Opal. He rubbed his eyes. "Why did you ask me here today?"

Her reply was quick. "To see if you have come across any correspondence that would confirm an affair. I already have scientific confirmation with these reports, but I'd like to add personal verification as well. Have you come across any personal correspondence or diary entries that would support this finding?"

Ash's frown deepened. "I have not because no documents of that sort exist."

Opal leaned in. "With all due respect, you read the report. You saw that my DNA has no genetic connection to Griffin Quill. For whatever reason or circumstance, someone else fathered Pearl Quill."

Ash rubbed the bridge of his nose. "When are you publishing this nonsense?"

"Tomorrow. It's the lead story in the morning edition. I was hoping you could be my source to confirm that Faith might have had a motive to have an affair."

"Motive?" he whispered.

Opal grinned. "Griffin was twenty-six when he married a fourteen-year-old, Faith."

Ash's face went red. "What are you suggesting?"

"I'm asking if Griffin Quill and William Kramer struck some type of deal."

Ash rubbed his temple with his fingers. "What type of deal would Faith Kramer's father strike with Griffin Quill?"

"I found a shipping log stating that Griffin bought a ticket to return to Germany on July 17, 1877. He was Kramer's prized manager of The Claire Hotel; Kramer certainly did not want to lose his number one man. Three days after the ticket was purchased, Griffin and Faith married, and his name never appeared on the ship's boarding docket as having sailed back to Germany."

Ash chortled a laugh. "Ha! You think William Kramer sold his daughter to Griffin Quill in a business deal."

Opal hesitated. "*Sold* is too strong of a word. Do you think it possible that Kramer sweetened the deal to persuade Griffin to stay in America and not board that ship?"

Ash deflected her assertion with another laugh.

"And now you are the expert on the Quill family? I can assure you, Mrs. Schatz, that Griffin and Faith loved each other." He pointed his finger toward the castle nestled just offshore. "That monument is proof of his love for her."

Opal shot back. "And Faith died before ever seeing it."

Ash reluctantly nodded. "True. But you will recall that Griffin's health deteriorated quickly after her sudden death. He died of a broken heart. Everyone knows this."

Opal tilted her head. "I'm just trying to determine if their marriage was indeed the true love story everyone knows and loves, or if, perhaps, fairy dust has been thrown into our eyes to hide the truth. Did an assault lead to the third child? Did she have an affair? Did she love two men?"

Ash sat back and chose his words carefully. "Have you ever been in love, Mrs. Schatz? Really in love, a love that absorbs every molecule of your being?"

Opal felt her birthmark burn as her face went flush. A drop of sweat dripped down her back. "Yes. I have known real love."

Before Ash could continue, Opal cleared her throat and read from her notes. "It is documented that Faith Quill's death was due to a weak heart, but have you ever heard about the other common rumor, the one about the diet pills."

The slam of Ash's hand on the table made Opal jerk backward.

"That's enough!" Ash waved his hand spasmodically to trivialize her suggestion. "I now understand why you invited me here today." He wobbled when he stood.

"You should know that history is often more complex than it seems," Opal said.

But Ash Burton was done talking. He stood up straight, and, with newfound stability and deftness, trekked out of Opal's office right by her and out the front door.

By the time Opal reached the sidewalk, Ash Burton was halfway down the block. When he turned the corner at Alex Bay's Public Library, Opal was sure of one thing: she had made Ash Burton cry.

CHAPTER 3

Opal replayed the interview with Ash Burton while pouring her third cup of coffee, and again when microwaving leftovers for lunch, and again while dropping off a deposit bag at the Alex Bay bank just before it closed.

Opal stared at the design mock-ups for the next two upcoming editions of *The River Gazette*. The two headlines were similar in size but carried a different message – *DNA Results Rock Alex Bay* and *The Case of the Missing Teens: Twenty-Five Years Later*. For a town whose biggest stories over the last six months were the collapse of an abandoned grain silo at Joe Deakin's pasture that killed his prize bull and the birth of Butch and Sissy's triplets in the spring, these articles were considered bombshell material.

Located on the St. Lawrence River, ninety minutes north of Syracuse, NY, and ninety minutes south of Ottawa, Canada, Alexandria Bay draws half a million tourists and history buffs to this northern Adirondack region of New York State from Memorial Day to Labor Day. They arrive in droves like moths to flames. The scatterings of small islands dot the mile-wide St. Lawrence River, creating a liquid border between the States and Canada. From an aerial view, it was easy to see the draw. The luxurious remoteness and picturesque sunsets drew the wealthy industrialists of Manhattan in the late 1800s. They built lavish, secluded retreats away from the gray and noisy traffic of city life after a train line reduced the trip between the locations to just three hours.

The very tension in Opal's veins tonight was that same forceful rhythm that had recently propelled her career onward and upward. *The River Gazette's* circulation numbers were up twelve percent; the profit line was on a similar trajectory. Of the six articles she had published about Quill Castle history, the Associated Press picked up all of them while Reuters and UPI ran half. For the first time in her career, Opal Schatz's articles were not limited only to subscribers in teeny, tiny Alexandria Bay, population 1,100; instead, they were being zipped around the globe to various time zones and different cultures. There was no question that readers were lured into the intrigue of Quill Castle, considering *The River Gazette's* newest followers on its Instagram page were from California, Germany, and Dubai.

At her desk, Opal evaluated the digital sycamore tree on her computer screen and dragged its trunk two millimeters to the left. She had designed the page to dangle the names of Quill heirs from brown branches, a visual representation of the DNA results. "And that's a wrap," she said to herself.

A click on a corner X closed the screen and revealed a screensaver photo of her staff – all two of them. They were people she defended as ruthlessly and as often as necessary.

"You're haggling," Opal told the newspaper owner.

"I did not approve their raises," Peter Welling said.

"I know that. I did," Opal said.

"As the owner of twenty newspapers across the country, including yours, let me remind you that I am the only one with the authority to do that."

"Pete. Save it. I was in little, tiny pieces after Daniel died, and you know that. Mitch and Roxie kept the paper running for weeks, maybe months, with little to no help from me."

Pete groaned. "They are the only reporters in the company who don't have set hours, the only ones who don't punch a timecard."

"And it will stay that way as long as I'm at the helm. Let's do lunch soon, Pete."

His silence signaled his defeat. "Yes. Lunch. Soon." Click.

Simply put, Opal loved Mitch Thompson and Roxie Sataro, and while they might not be as savvy as reporters from major newspapers, they knew when to talk and when to listen.

Born, bred and settled in Jefferson County, former Alexandria Bay track star Mitch Thompson covered sports. During tourist season, he split his time between writing for the paper and running Castle Gifts, a seasonal shop on the main drag that banked a hundred thousand dollars before the opening September bell of the school year. Still tall, lanky, and solidly into his forties, summer signaled a break from visiting fields for his five sons' high school sporting events. When Mitch said, "my wife is a saint", everyone knew he wasn't lying.

Roxie Sataro, though, was another story altogether. She had come into Opal's life based on chance, in what Opal considered a sheer stroke of luck. After learning that her financial aid had fallen through for her last semester of grad school at Syracuse University, she had hopped on Interstate 81 and driven north, pedal to the metal, until she ran out of gas in front of *The River Gazette*. That was six years ago.

Now at thirty, Roxie never granted her family's wish to return to Portugal; instead, she morphed into an Alex Bay transplant by developing a fascination for the ebb and flow of local politics and small-town community groups. She tolerated writing articles about local service organizations donating funds to a food kitchen and snapped photos at annual fundraising dinners, while waiting for the other shoe to drop – for the secretary or treasurer of those groups to fall under investigation for missing funds. One thing had become clear to Opal: Roxie had a nose for news and thrived when embroiled in the chaotic thick of it.

Opal was surprised to see Roxie walk into the lobby, all five feet of her, looking like she was ready to cheer on the Blue Jays in her baseball jersey, shorts and sneakers. A pencil held up her jet-black hair in a sloppy bun, which complemented her olive skin making her look unassumingly beautiful.

"Hey," Roxie said, dropping a gym bag on the floor and plopping herself into a chair across from her boss.

"What brings you by so late?"

"Wanted to see if you were ready for your sister-in-law to shit herself tomorrow morning when she reads the article."

"I almost called her to warn her. Faith's affair removed her and an entire line of Quill lineage."

"I suggest you move to the next county before dawn, and I'm sure Howard already has a suitcase packed by the door," she said. "I'd like to be a fly on the wall watching her read tomorrow's front page."

Opal tapped the table with her index finger. "Claudine agreed to the stipulations. She knew the results would be published."

Roxie giggled. "Living in a small town anywhere means preserving oneself behind a mask," she said. "A very astute Doris Lessing said that."

"Well, I'm about to rip off that mask with the morning edition."

Roxie chuckled. "Listen. You're the one who told me that Claudine Schatz has always seen herself as a queen among the serfs. Tomorrow, your sister-in-law finds out that she is nothing but a hard-working drummer who landed in the ashcan like the rest of us, that she is simply another Willy Loman." Roxie used her hands to mime an explosion over her head.

Opal reflected on her morning interview. "I seem to be blowing up reality for a lot of people. My interview with Ash Burton ended with him leaving in tears."

"Your research is solid. Besides, it confirms what I have always known you as."

"What's that?"

"A heartbreaker."

Opal rolled her eyes. "It has been an emotional week. We've all had Brian Annetti and Patty Flanagan on our minds. Twenty-five years. Hard to believe they've never been found."

"Covering that story must have been tough," Roxie said.

Opal shook her head. "Writing the articles was easy. I relied on police and FBI press releases to put together the timeline of their disappearance. With no witnesses, no evidence, and no bodies, there wasn't much to report."

Roxie nodded. "What do you remember most about their disappearance?"

Opal sat back. "I remember sitting in the police station waiting for a press conference to begin when they led the parents to the podium to beg the public for information." Opal leaned forward. "They moved as though they were in slow motion, like they were trapped inside some sort of time continuum. They were unable to move forward yet unable to go back."

Roxie's voice was soft. "And they've been stuck in that continuum for twenty-five years." .

CHAPTER 4

Wanting to put her long day to rest, Opal headed home to wash the thin sheen of humidity from her skin. The cool shower slowed the spinning emotions in her head – shame for making Ash Burton cry, anxiety for rattling family lines, anguish for next week's anniversary edition featuring the missing teens.

But the albatross around her neck had always been Daniel's sudden death. He wasn't supposed to collapse into his bowl of oatmeal and peaches while reading the morning edition, and she wasn't supposed to get a call from Claudine saying he was dead. Although a year had passed, she still half-expected a casual text from Daniel asking whether she wanted sushi or tacos for dinner. What she wished for she knew was impossible – for Daniel to live again until she gave him permission to die.

Was that really too much to ask?

Opal slipped into a thin nightgown, shivering as cool air from a floor vent reached her skin. She then slipped off her wedding ring and set it atop her bureau. She massaged the deep welt on her ring finger before sliding the gold and diamond band back on. Opal stood there repeating the Miyagi-like process – ring on, ring off, ring on, ring off – wondering if she would ever be able to live her life without it. Without him. The ring, which had claimed its rightful spot on her finger four months after her high school graduation in 1970, had become part of her identity.

The warmth she felt when she returned the ring into its regular groove turned sour when she locked eyes on the top drawer. A mantra of phrases whispered in her head: *Do not open that drawer. Do not read the letter. You must stop.*

A low moan rolled in her throat. Her stomach lurched, bending her forward in physical pain. It was guilt she felt, a guilt pounding on her conscience like a hammer on an anvil. She sucked in deep breaths, reaching out and grabbing the stable bureau to balance herself upright. And with her recovery, as though she had learned nothing, Opal pulled open the drawer and gently withdrew a worn envelope. Scrawled on the front in blue ink were three distinct words – *My Dearest Opal*.

Her past attempts to distance herself from that letter had failed. The time she tucked it under a flap of rug in the back corner of her closet only to find herself reading it by flashlight while Daniel slept just feet away. The time she sent it to the street in a recycling bin full of newspapers only to sneak out in the moonlight and haul the stack back into the garage. And even after Daniel discovered her there with ink-stained fingers and asked her what the hell she was doing, she found her lie came easy. "I promised Bree an extra copy of the paper with the article about Enzo's promotion."

Daniel had merely scratched his head, yawned, and went back to bed.

He had trusted her, and it was Daniel's unwavering loyalty that made her guilt so raw. Like an addict craving her next hit, she removed the letter, opened it, and read its simple directions that she had followed so perfectly as an eighteen-year-old, over forty years ago.

CHAPTER 5

In the pre-dawn hours of the morning, questions pelted Opal's brain like hail on a window: Did Griffin Quill know his youngest child was illegitimate? Did Faith's affair have anything to do with her sudden death? How will Claudine make me pay for humiliating her? Will they ever find Brian Annetti and Patty Flanagan? She lay there, mulling over those questions, until adrenaline eliminated the possibility of more sleep.

"That does it." She threw the covers back and climbed out of bed.

Ten minutes later, shrouded in the darkness before dawn, Opal cut through the park and headed toward the marina. When she spotted her boat in its usual slip, she stopped. The embers of a distant memory fanned themselves to life.

She felt Daniel's warm whisper against her ear. "Keep your eyes closed," he said. Her body had leaned back into his chest, an alcove seemingly carved for only her.

"Mom! Don't peek," Ruby had said, her young voice trying to sound authoritative and firm at the critical moment of this father-daughter secret mission.

"I can't see a thing with this blindfold," Opal had assured her. "Are people staring at us? Does it look like I'm being kidnapped?"

Ruby giggled.

Opal had played up the moment by feigning ignorance. "Where have you taken me? Are we still in Alex Bay?"

Ruby directed her father. "Don't take off the blindfold until I say. Daniel loosened the knot as Ruby counted down. "Three. Two. One."

The thin fabric fell to the ground, and Opal focused her eyes toward the river.

"Ta-da!" Ruby had squealed.

"Happy birthday," Daniel had said, kissing Opal's cheek.

Opal stared at a large white boat bobbing in the water, its two silver metal tubes keeping it securely afloat. An oversized red bow hung from the stern's railing just above black lettering that spelled out the vessel's name: *My Gem I*.

"You bought me a pontoon boat," she said, dumbfounded.

Daniel slid his hand around Opal's waist, then nestled it into the small of her back. "I did."

Little Ruby frowned. "The boat is for all of us, right?"

Daniel patted her head. "Anyone who makes her bed every day and does the dishes and takes out the trash can use the boat."

"Dad!"

"Let's get a look at this beauty." Opal stepped aboard, taking in its shape, the control console, the deep wicker storage benches filled with life jackets. She opened the seat and took one out, securing the device over her head and its straps around her waist.

"Mom, you don't have to wear a life jacket when we are docked."

Opal reached into the storage space a second time. "You're right. I'll wear two."

With the engine murmuring softly, Opal maneuvered the newest version of the original – the *My Gem IV* – out of the boat slip and onto the quiet river, the place she felt closest to Daniel. Mounted at the tip of the bow, revolving red and green navigation lights led the way. She eased the throttle forward to pick up speed, just as the first strands of yellow and orange broke the horizon. It wasn't until she passed under the region's grand turquoise expansion bridge that she felt free.

Opal needed the river. The warm wind quieted her questions, her doubts, her guilt, as she watched the shoreline sleep before yawning itself awake for a bustling day of tourist season. Growing up here, Opal knew that a few hours still needed to pass until waiters served fancy drinks to relaxed patrons at riverside restaurants, until speedboats would pull squealing tubers from braided ropes, until green and orange striped parasails suspended their cargo high above the blue current. They were still hours away from long lines of cars clogging I-81. The highway's new signage encouraged travelers to stay at the renovated Bijou House, the original Thousand Islands

House, and to snap a photo under the *Welcome to the Thousand Islands: Home of Quill Castle* banner at the center of town.

Those managing Airbnbs or Vrbos were often up early documenting any property damage committed by drunk patrons during the night. About a quarter of Alex-Bayers spend most of May prettying up their backyards, stringing up solar lights and sanitizing hot tubs, all with the hopes of enhancing their profiles on vacation rental websites. The crème de la crème properties provide complementary golf carts – a staple form of transportation for locals – for late-night trips downtown for a 7Eleven Slurpee or a Tats 'n Brews cold beer. The decision to cater to would-be-tourists was a moot point for those staring at college tuition bills or alimony payment stubs. Business owners learned to plan new events yearly to keep the area interesting and fresh for repeat vacationers. This year, visitors can have lunch with a pirate at St. Larry's Riverside Lounge or receive a skull and crossbones manicure at Castle Creations Beauty Spa.

But most will board the tried-and-true Rhineland ferry to visit two of the fourteen castles in New York State – Singer and Quill – which sit on their own islands within the extended archipelago of the Thousand Islands. The structures had been built during the first few years of the twentieth century, a time of unprecedented wealth in America.

Renowned architect Ernest Flagg, whose top projects included the Chrysler Building in New York City, had designed and oversaw the construction of Singer Castle as commissioned by Frederick Gilbert Bourne, then-president of the Singer Manufacturing Company.

Although it resided on the ominous-sounding Dark Island, the towering structure was considered the only 'working' castle on the St. Lawrence River since it was completed and occupied by builders and industrialists at the heyday of Gilded Age.

But it was Starr Island – a five-acre speck of land just off the shore of Alex Bay – that attracted the most tourists. On it, Quill Castle rose six stories into the sky, standing proud with her burnished copper turrets, crafted stone parapets, and gray-tiled roof. Her fifty thousand square feet held eighty-eight rooms with specific areas designed for the enjoyment of the Quill children, including a bowling alley, in-ground swimming pool and full-sized theater. Griffin Quill aimed to construct a fairy tale castle for his cherished wife and children. The grand structure was surrounded by expansive, curated Italian gardens highlighting red, yellow and purple blooms planted in patterns that complemented its limestone archways, iron gates and stone fountains.

But most visitors walking the grounds, from eager history buffs to self-proclaimed romantics, were simply intoxicated by the lure of historical heartbreak and tragedy embedded in the stately structure. Most of the castle's tour docents repeatedly clarified that many rumors swirling about the castle's construction weren't rumors at all. Yes, Griffin Quill had used thousands of pounds of dynamite to reshape the island into its current star shape. Yes, he had commissioned the building of a full-size Rhineland-inspired castle as a surprise Valentine's Day gift for his wife. Yes, Faith had died just weeks before the castle's completion, never having seen the structure. And when docents revealed the terrible fact of Faith's sudden death in 1904, they pointed to strategically placed tissues so guests could dab their teary eyes at the tragedy of it all.

During tours, a screen flashed black and white video clips of the castle's restoration while a deep voice explained the historical highlights of the impressive structure. Locals knew the history: upon learning of Faith's sudden death, Griffin immediately halted construction, and the castle was abandoned in that sorry, incomplete state. It remained unfinished and vacant for seventy years, falling victim to harsh elements, selfish vandals, and curious teenagers, all in equal severity. Bitter cold winds had slammed lake effect snow into its corroding turret peaks and cracked oak millwork, vandals used crowbars to remove large sections of Italian Carrara marble floors and to smash imported stained-glass skylights. High school teens had often risked the short trip from the mainland to build bonfires, smoke pot and drink vodka stolen from their sleeping parents' liquor cabinets. It wasn't until a comprehensive renovation project was greenlit in 1974 that a resident groundsman was hired to live at the castle. Public tours began three years later.

Opal's thoughts shifted to the morning newspapers that were currently curled up on front porches, waiting to be read with a cup of coffee. She eased off the throttle while mentally reviewing the proactive steps she took with those who volunteered their DNA for the article. Maybe having arranged for them to receive copies of their DNA reports, while assuring them with handwritten notes that no other copies of their data existed, would reduce the number of calls and complaints she would receive. As she steered *My Gem IV* to circle Quill Castle for the return trip home, she thought to herself, maybe it wouldn't be so bad.

She was wrong.

CHAPTER 6

Addie Muldowney got the ball rolling. "My grandmother told us we had Quill blood in us, and you're saying Granny Mae was a liar? How dare you!" Her voice quivered in grief and anger.

"I'm only saying that the report you have is accurate," Opal squeezed in just before Addie hung up on her.

The next call was from James Buckingham, the Alexandria Bay School Superintendent. He didn't mince words. "Now you listen to me. I have reviewed my DNA report with my attorneys, and we agree that if my information is used in any additional capacity, your career and the future of the newspaper will be over."

"Mr. Buckingham," Opal said, ignoring his threat. "I only printed that you were not a direct descendant of the Quill family." She chose her next words carefully. "No one else will know." She had intended for her words to reassure him that the newspaper would not reveal he had another son out there, judging by Mr. Buckingham's voice, Mrs. Buckingham knew nothing about.

"You'll be hearing from my lawyers." Another click.

The pressure or threat of lawsuits was not new to Opal. At least once a month, typically after she published the DUI/DWI arrests in the Police Blotter, promises of litigation rang in her ear like the clanging opening bell on Wall Street.

"You can't print that," said Walter Meezly, Alex Bay's Democratic mayor. "The Republicans have the majority, for Christ's sake. They could vote me out."

"Wally, it's far more likely they would vote you out if you had hurt someone when driving around town with a .16 blood alcohol level. You could have killed someone."

"Bitch." Click.

Wally's call did not bother her any more than the others; she had grown thick skin long ago. But it was the lack of one call that left Opal tapping a pencil on her desk. No call from Claudine.

CHAPTER 7

The blond bank clerk rushed into the Alexandria Bank manager's office doorway; her breath was urgent. "A woman just crashed her golf cart into the building."

Enzo Kennedy did not hesitate. "Call 9-1-1." He brushed his chest against her thin torso, his fingers barely grazing her hips before sprinting through the lobby and out the front door.

In the morning heat, he struggled to push his way through the wide circle of spectators that had formed around a mad woman busily jerking her dented golf cart back and forth over piles of torn newspapers. He looked left, seeing *The River Gazette's* coin-operated honor box toppled over in a heap, its contents splayed across the sidewalk. And when he looked back at the driver, he could only roll his eyes. Each time the Jefferson County Fair Peach Pie Champion shifted in reverse, her rear fender collided with the building, sending bricks tumbling down into a heap.

"What the hell, Claudine?" Enzo put his hands on his hips. His dress slacks, red tie and white short-sleeved shirt did nothing to downplay his greasy comb-over.

She did not hear him. Her bony form was hunched over the steering wheel, her teeth bared in unleashed rage. Claudine's stringy strands of gray were disheveled, sloppily pulled back into a crooked clip. The town knew she started baking at six each morning, but today, she didn't even take the time to remove her kitchen apron before launching the attack.

Approaching sirens scattered the crowd and a patrol car parked on the curb. With swift movements, the police chief exited his vehicle, jumped onto the moving golf cart, and pulled the key out of the ignition.

Police Chief Hollis Walker leaned in towards her ear and whispered. "Get ahold of yourself, Claudine." To the rest of the crowd, he offered assurances. "Everything is fine. Nothing more to see here, folks. Let's move on."

Locking his arm in hers, he guided Claudine off the cart and toward the bank entrance.

"You can use my office," Enzo said.

Claudine sat in an office chair with her arms folded across her chest. "I want her arrested for disturbing the peace."

"You want who arrested?"

"My sister-in-law of whose name I refuse to speak."

Hollis shot Enzo a confused look.

Enzo passed Hollis his copy of the morning newspaper and watched him read the headline at the top – *No Heirs About It: Local DNA Tests Break Quill Family Lines*. The photo under the headline showed Opal sitting on the steps of Quill Castle's grand staircase holding a picture of the Quill family crest – a capital Q encased within a star.

Hollis could not help but smirk. "Opal did not disturb the peace. You are the one facing charges. To start with …"

Enzo interrupted. "The bank does not wish to press charges. The damage is minor."

Claudine didn't back down. "Then I want her arrested for harassment."

"How is she harassing you?"

Claudine leaned toward the Chief. "She is using that publication to destroy my reputation, my legacy," She grabbed the newspaper out of Enzo's hand and clutched it in her fist. "This is the glorification of trash." She threw it to the floor.

"I do not have control over what the paper publishes," Hollis said.

"This is not the first time, though," Claudine said more urgently. "I filed a formal complaint the last time she did this, back before you became chief."

Hollis frowned. "I'm sorry to say I don't know about that, but I assure you I will look into it."

Claudine huffed.

Hollis's cell phone chimed. He read the text and stood. "I have to go."

Enzo met him at the door and kept his voice low. "I'll call Howard to come to get her."

Hollis nodded. "Thanks, Enzo. Looks like I owe you yet another one." The two men shook hands. On Hollis's way out, Enzo patted him on the back.

Claudine's voice was bitter. "There is no need to call my husband. Howard doesn't understand things the way I do."

Enzo picked up the newspaper. "Bree told me about the article this morning." He snapped the crumpled pages straight. "Sounds like sour grapes to me."

Claudine sprang from her chair with such speed that Enzo took a step back. "How dare you. When I tell Howard what you said to me, he will come down here and…"

Enzo held up his right hand, smiling. "Shake my hand?"

His willingness to mock her faded when he saw the jagged pink scar running between his thumb and index finger. He slid the marked hand into his pocket, turning his gaze toward his shoes.

Claudine was too busy whisking by him and out the door to notice.

Enzo threw the newspaper on his desk and closed his office door, his fingers turning the deadbolt to the locked position. He hurried behind his desk, twisted closed the window blinds, and sat in his worn leather chair. Using the hunt-and-peck method, he typed his password, pausing only to wipe a drop of saliva from his mouth in anticipation.

Three computer screens formed a half-circle arc on his desk. One by one, each came to life displaying live surveillance video feeds from cameras perched high above the bank lobby. Each camera was zoomed in on a female employee's chest or ass. Enzo grinned.

When Enzo's eyes momentarily landed on his framed wedding photo of himself and Bree, he tilted their smiling faces forward until they were flat on the desk. He returned his focus to the live images, running his index finger over his lips and chin before setting his hand on his crotch.

CHAPTER 8

"The FBI?"

"Nope."

"The State Police?"

"Nope."

Hollis sat across the table from Opal in *The River Gazette's* lobby. "I give up. Who discovered the dagger was stolen?" He set a white bakery bag on the table and pushed it toward Opal.

"A curator from the Metropolitan Museum of Art," Opal said, opening the bag and pulling out a glazed blueberry scone.

"What?" he laughed. "How?"

"She was vacationing here with her family. She had read Mitch's article about the Celtic dagger Claudine bought from an estate sale; she thought the photo looked familiar and did some investigating. Turns out it was stolen about a century ago."

"That explains why she thinks you are harassing her," Hollis said.

Opal got up and plucked through a stack of newspapers in the corner. "I'm sure I have an extra copy of the article." She pulled one out near the bottom. "Here it is." She opened it for Hollis to see.

Hollis raised his eyebrows. He eyed the front-page color photo of the ancient, jeweled knife, its grip and guard bedazzled with emeralds and rubies above a silver blade; it glittered with radiance. The picture also showed Claudine standing at her kitchen island, pretending to use the dagger to cut one of her home-baked peach pies.

"She found *that* at an estate sale?" Hollis asked.

Opal explained. "She bought an old trunk that contained scraped pans, wooded frames, spools of gift ribbon and a smattering of other random items. Claudine found it lying at the very bottom under a layer of packing paper. I think she paid fifty bucks for the trunk."

"How long ago was that?"

"Over a year ago," she said. "A few months before Daniel died."

"How did the story end up in the paper?" Hollis asked.

"You know that Daniel taught history at Jefferson Community. After he read through his semester stack of student research papers, he always passed the top essay on to Mitch for a follow-up human-interest piece. You know as well as I do that the newspaper doesn't always run positive stories about college students," Opal said, sharing a grin with Hollis. "Let's just say it helped build a relationship between our office and the academic community. But that's not the worst part."

Hollis rubbed his temple. "It gets worse?"

Opal nodded. "The museum was so happy that Claudine willingly agreed to return the dagger to its collection that they offered to put it on loan here in Alex Bay for one year so tourists and residents could get one last look. It's due to be returned to New York City next month."

Hollis thought about that. "I think I saw it a few weeks ago at my cousin's wedding. Is it mounted on the wall at St. Elizabeth's?"

"Yep. That was it," Opal said.

Hollis grinned. "I don't understand why it was a bad idea to display the dagger in a church. They have a security system there."

"It wasn't a bad idea to display the dagger in a church, but it was a bad idea to display the dagger in *Claudine's church* so that she can sit in a pew every Sunday, listen to the word of God, and stare at the jeweled dagger that she once believed was hers."

Hollis's phone vibrated. He motioned that he needed privacy, so Opal pointed for him to take her office in the back.

Seeing that photo again took Opal back to the day she saw the dagger for the first time at Howard and Claudine's house.

Opal remembered walking hand in hand with Daniel on a cool day to snap some photographs of Claudine's great find. When they came around the corner of Water Street, they saw Howard was clipping the bushes on the front lawn with hand sheers. Daniel set his hand on his brother's shoulder, startling him before giving him a firm handshake.

"What brings you by?" Howard said.

"I'd like to take some photos of your dagger to show my class," Daniel said.

"Sure." Howard undid the top button of his jeans and pretended to lower the zipper.

Opal shook her head. "You two will never change." She headed up the front porch stairs and into the house. "I'll take some photos in the living room."

The brothers watched the screen door close behind her.

Howard spoke the sentence they both thought: "She is still beautiful."

Daniel nodded, letting the comment pass.

"Claudine is at a League luncheon at River Rocks Café," Howard said. "Peach muffins are on the counter, baked fresh this morning."

"She's already getting ready for the fair?" Daniel asked.

"She is always getting ready for the fair," Howard said, patting his belly.

Opal called out from a screened window. "Hey. How much did this set you back?"

Howard led the duo up the stairs and into the house. The moment the men joined Opal in the living room, Daniel let out a long whistle.

"Holy shit. Would you look at that."

"Two grand," Howard said to Opal. "And some change."

The prized dagger was mounted on the wall behind a protective fiberglass case. A spotlight affixed to the ceiling streamed a constant beam onto its silver blade.

Using her phone, Opal took photos from different angles.

"What do you need with those?" Howard asked.

Daniel answered. "I kick off the research project on Monday."

"Oh boy," Howard said. "What's the topic this year?"

"Weapons of torture."

"That tops last year's Famous Bank Heists, for sure."

"I'm including close-quarter combat on my list of options, so these pictures should help spur some interest from the class. In a few weeks, you should expect a hungover teenager standing on your porch asking for an interview."

Opal leaned in close to examine the object. "Have you ever had it appraised?" Opal asked. "I heard *Antiques Roadshow* is visiting Syracuse this winter."

"No need to pay for an expert when I'm married to one."

Chief Walker returned to the lobby just as Mitch limped into the office, his foot in a black high-tech therapy boot. White gauze and paper tape were stuck to Mitch's temple. He wore a turquoise *I Love Alex Bay* t-shirt from his shop, cargo shorts and one flip-flop on his good foot. He sank into his office chair at his desk.

Opal grinned. "Which kid is responsible for that?"

"Who else?" Mitch said.

"Henry," said Opal and Hollis in unison.

Mitch's hands waved in the air to illustrate the messy details. "I *thought* we would do a father-son project by adding some storage space for boats onto the back of the marina. And I *thought* Henry was listening to me when I told him to kneel on a two-by-four before I walked across it. Turns out the only thing he was listening to was music in his earbuds and now I have eight stitches in my head and a sprained ankle."

"I could always arrest him," Hollis offered, grinning.

"Trust me," Mitch said. "You'd bring him back before lunch. You looking for Roxie? I know she had some questions about the Annetti-Flanagan case."

Hollis shook his head. "No. I found her earlier. We're all set. I'm here because I've just learned that Claudine had previously filed a complaint about the dagger article." He held up the old issue. "She is claiming a pattern of harassing behavior from the newspaper against her."

"Are you fucking kidding me?" Mitch said, slamming his hand on the desk. He struggled to get up but slumped back down in surrender to his ankle pain. "She is just pissed that the paper de-throned her majesty."

Hollis held up his hands. "You can all relax. While I must record her complaints, I don't have to act on them."

"Glad to hear our police chief has common sense," said Opal. "Thank you."

Mitch wheeled his chair forward. "You were down south for a couple of years. Glad you moved back?" He dropped his head, regretting his question.

"I was glad I could spend Dad's last days with him. And while I did love living in a big city, Mom sure makes a mean meatloaf up here, so..."

Opal patted Hollis's arm.

Another beep from his phone drew the Chief's attention. He stood to leave. At the door, he turned back. "I know there are many obvious differences between small towns and big cities, but each place settles disputes quite differently. Cities use guns. Small towns tend to settle them with something else."

"What's that?" Mitch asked.

"Revenge."

CHAPTER 9

Ash Burton's library was a small rectangular room tucked in the back corner of a two-story Cape Cod located on the outskirts of Alexandria Bay. On three sides, tall bookcases held an impressive line of books dedicated to New York State history. His bulky wooden desk held three books written about the Quill family – *In Search of the Lost Story*, *The Unfinished Dream*, *The Love Story of Quill Castle*. Each volume had torn pieces of paper sticking up from the pages, physical markers for information or details Ash wanted to visit again.

The walls, decorated with several walnut-framed Impressionist paintings emphasizing blue water, lavender flowers and soft sunny days, supported a cathedral ceiling. Its wallpaper – a Wedgewood blue background with overlays of white hydrangeas, roses, and dogwood blooms – was a lovely reminder that his home was on the Alex Bay Historical Home Tour for a reason.

Ash sat in a wood-carved high-back chair, thinking of how Opal Schatz had convincingly pierced hole after hole into a story he had dedicated a good portion of his life accepting as undeniable truth.

As the tall grandfather clock in a corner chimed twice, Vivian Burton peeked inside the library. "Penny for your thoughts."

"Come in, please," Ash said.

Vivian had short gray hair and warm green eyes that had the power to diffuse Ash's angst instantly. She wore navy cotton slacks, and her torso was wrapped in a muted blue and white patterned flannel shirt. Despite a noticeable limp on her right side, she steadily carried a tray that held the fixings for their afternoon tea – kettle, cups, saucers, spoons, cream.

Ash stood up and took the tray from her. "You shouldn't have gone through the trouble, Viv. Let me help you." He set the tray on a square coffee table, and they sat across from each other on cushioned chairs.

Vivian knew her husband well enough to know it was better to let him start the conversation when he was in an agitated state. By the time she poured tea in their porcelain cups, Ash blurted out the details of his morning visit with Opal Schatz.

"She was obnoxious, Viv. Absolutely obnoxious."

"What did she say?" Vivian listened, sipping her tea.

"That Faith Quill had an affair," Ash said. "That Faith's father could have arranged her marriage to Griffin."

Vivian nodded. "I read the newspaper article earlier. The DNA data certainly seems to support the affair theory."

He wiped his nose, swatting her comment away. "DNA evidence is not always reliable," he shot back.

Vivian smiled. "I bet you already have a plan on how to proceed."

Ash ran his knuckles over his knees. "I'm heading to the county Historical Society tomorrow to look through employment records, photos, receipts, and purchase orders related to the Quill family business."

"Maybe you will find something to prove yourself right."

Ash sighed. "I just want something to prove Opal Schatz wrong."

CHAPTER 10

Loud twangs of banjo strings bounced through the open door when Roxie arrived at *The River Gazette* for the staff meeting regarding the disappearance of Brian Annetti and Patty Flanagan.

Roxie wiped the sweat from her forehead.

"How hot is it out there?" Opal asked.

"About a hundred."

"How many people are at Music at the Park?" Mitch said.

Roxie calculated an estimate. "About a hundred."

"What's the average age of the crowd?" he said.

"About a hundred."

Roxie grabbed a small basketball from her desk and shot it at a plastic hoop attached to a ceiling tile; she sank the shot, signaling the start of the meeting. Opal, Mitch, and Roxie gathered around the table, each leafing through their notes.

Opal began. "Since it's the twenty-fifth anniversary of their disappearance, we will likely get national coverage. If you get any calls from other news agencies, take a message, get a name and number, and text me. Corporate wants to know who calls and what they are asking."

Mitch and Roxie nodded.

Opal shared the challenge of their task. "You know as well as I do that putting a fresh spin on an unsolved mystery that has had no new leads or developments for twenty-five years is tough. Any ideas on a different approach?"

Mitch responded. "I spoke with the new director of the local Underwater Rescue Team last week. He said a missing body could theoretically travel from the St. Lawrence River to the Atlantic Ocean without being found. He admitted that the likelihood of that happening was low because a body could easily become lodged in a drainage pipe or debris below the islands' surface."

"Is that what he thinks happened to Patty and Brian?" Opal said.

"Off the record, yes," Mitch said. "On the record, he said the police or FBI should review the entire case, that fresh eyes might find fresh leads."

Roxie moaned. "A red canoe. A backpack. Gum wrappers. An unopened condom. That's it." She readjusted the pencil in her hair. "Time and technology can't change the truth. Everyone knows they drowned. Why can't they legally be declared dead?"

"Because of the parents," Opal said. "They would have to file paperwork asking for that designation. For whatever reason, they can't do it."

Roxie read from a page in her notepad. "Brian's mother died of breast cancer last year. His dad, Luke, lives in Buffalo. I left him a voicemail message. Patty's parents moved to England three years ago. My contact numbers for each have mailboxes that have never been set up."

"Crickets," Mitch said.

"I left a message for the FBI Regional Office in Syracuse," Opal said. "Her secretary said I should get a callback tomorrow morning."

Roxie flipped a page. "I'm interviewing Brian's English teacher and the current high school principal tonight, and I heard that someone there was planning a memorial service."

Opal swiveled her computer screen toward her colleagues. "Here's the design for the weekend front page."

Mitch and Roxie ignored the empty lined boxes still waiting for article copy and stared instead at two color photos of Patty Flanagan and Brian Annetti, their heads tilted slightly to the right, most likely at the direction of the photographer. Brian's dark curls peeked out from his cap; his grin was one of confidence, saying he had his entire future ahead of him and planned on making the most of it. Patty's long, blond hair rested over each shoulder; she wore her grandmother's pearls around her slender neck. It was the blue burst of her eyes that mesmerized the trio.

A beeping noise broke the spell.

Mitch looked at his phone. "Sorry guys. Gotta go." He winced as he stood, taking a moment to balance himself with the new contraption on his foot. "Henry locked himself out of the store."

Roxie and Opal shared a smile and watched him hobble out.

Opal was about to leave when Roxie asked her one more question. "You do not seem yourself. What gives?"

Opal sat back and covered her face with her hands, releasing a muffled moan. "Yesterday, I rattled Mr. Burton's cage by poking holes in his life's work. This morning, Claudine filed harassment claims against me and the newspaper. This afternoon, I'm trying to put a fresh spin on a story that's been dead for as long as the kids have been missing."

"I can't tell if you're complaining or not."

"Maybe that's the problem. I want to feel guilty. I should feel guilty."

"How *do* you feel?"

"Energized. Alive. Eager."

"So, you feel guilty for feeling good," Roxie quipped.

"I'm Catholic. I feel guilty about everything."

CHAPTER 11

Opal had been expecting an office supply delivery to arrive that afternoon but was surprised when the mail courier handed her a thin package before parking her metal dolly and unloading boxes. From the slim cardboard pocket, she slid out a stack of papers bound with brass clips. She sat down and read the thick document, running her knuckle back and forth over her birthmark while reading page after page. A book contract! Upon reading the last words on the last page, she blew the air out of her lungs. A single thought overtook her thoughts – *I need Bree.*

Simply put, Bree Kennedy was to Opal Schatz what Rusty Ryan was to Danny Ocean, a best friend and partner in crime. She tucked the papers under her arm, flicked off the lights and stepped outside. With the heat of day beating down on her, Opal locked the office door and trekked down Central Avenue and up Main Street to share her secret with her best friend.

From the curb, the Kennedy home was modest and upscale. Opal followed the stone path to the backyard. Pink-tinted peonies bowed at her feet as she passed them by to climb the wooden stairs to the back deck. Over the years, Bree had transformed its floorboards and railings to resemble a pirate ship, complete with beams holding taut ropes connected to white sails that offered protection from the sun for outdoor guests. Purple morning glory blooms climbed Jacob's ladder toward the roof. Attached to the east side railing was a podium-like helm holding a ship's wooden steering wheel; a built-in shelf underneath held an impressive row of tall bottles that stood at attention for warm summer nights – rum, gin, vodka, merlot.

When Opal reached the top step, the tension in Opal's neck relaxed at the sight of Bree setting two frosted glasses beside a pitcher of lemonade on an iron-wrought table. Bree wore black shorts, lavender Crocs, and an extra-large white t-shirt that read *Art Teachers Are In It For The Monet* spelled out in sparkly red sequins across the front. When Bree spotted her best friend, she frowned, giving her best friend the once-over from head to toe.

"What's wrong?" Bree said.

"I wish Daniel were here."

"I know, love. Come, sit."

They sat across from each other and sipped lemonade, each trying not to stare at the thin package Opal had set on the table until Bree would have no more of that.

"What is that?" Bree nodded at the envelope.

"I got a call last week from an editor named Ebony White. She works for Butternut Hollow Books in New York."

"Ha! She's colors. You're gems," Bree quipped.

Opal did not smile.

"I'm sorry. Continue."

"She has been reading my articles about Quill Castle and thinks I should write a book."

"Hot damn!" Bree clapped her hands together in delight.

"Wait. There's more." Opal explained that a reporter from a magazine had interviewed her for a feature story for its July issue. "They called yesterday to confirm that I was sixty-three years old."

"I didn't think they could ask your age. Didn't you find that odd?"

Opal didn't answer.

"What magazine called you?" Bree persisted.

"AARP."

Bree let that register before barking out laughter that turned into a roar. She wiped her eyes before asking the obvious. "And you said yes, right?"

Opal fell silent. She struggled to find the right words. "Losing my husband a year ago, being interviewed by a national magazine, writing a book. It's too much, Bree."

Bree reached forward, taking Opal's hand into hers. "Listen. I retired too early. Instead of being Mrs. Kennedy and helping students paint self-portraits, I'm organizing a paint-by-numbers art class for Edvard Munch's *The Scream* on Fiona Wilder's fucking front lawn. I should have pushed myself. Just a little."

A nervous giggle escaped Opal's throat. "Whatever I decide, you know as well as I do that the expectations for my success and for my failure will be high." Tears welled in her eyes. "Bree, it makes me feel like I'm moving on."

Bree handed her a napkin. "Therein lies the rub. It's not about standing still or moving on. It's about deciding how you want your life defined. You know Daniel would have wanted that."

The two friends fell silent and looked out at a spectacular view of the St. Lawrence. The river was busy – speedboats zipped by pulling happy teens on inflated tubes, kayakers paddled along the shoreline, and small, motorized watercrafts jumped rolling wakes. All this while two tourist-packed ferries passed each other in opposite directions, one heading toward Quill Castle, the other toward shore, its whistle wailing to alert the ground crew to prepare for docking. As *The Rhineland* reached the platform, Bree and Opal waved at the couple at the helm. The man waved back. The woman did not.

"Ellie rides along with Mac now?" Opal asked.

"I heard he doesn't like leaving her alone anymore; she's too frail. I barely recognized her at mass last week." Bree shook her head. "We used to be so close, spent all our time together in high school, the four of us – you, me, Ellie and Claudine."

"The Quirky Quadruplets," Opal said.

Bree laughed. "Who gave us that nickname? Mrs. Cooper in Home Economics?"

"No. Mr. Weaver. Third-period math," Opal corrected.

"That's right," Bree said, nodding. "Then, right after graduation, I married Enzo, Ellie married Mac, Claudine married Howard, and you running off to elope with Daniel." Bree lifted her glass. "My God, that was forty-five years ago."

Opal nodded. "Right. Ruby was four when we moved back, and the town was so excited to learn that two best friends married the Schatz brothers, permanently linking Claudine and me."

Bree tipped her glass toward Opal. "Like a ball and chain."

CHAPTER 12

It was early evening, the time tourists started thinking about where to go for dinner that Bree Kennedy lay slouched in one of the many Adirondack chairs lining her deck. Opal had headed home earlier to reread the contract, leaving behind her copy of *The River Gazette* for Bree to read while savoring some cool drinks in the thick humidity. She sipped on her second (or third) gin and tonic, sniffing the tangy scents from The Castle Café's galley a few blocks away. Bree knew dinner was still hours after receiving Enzo's text stating he would be late. Again.

The Kennedy's agreed-upon retirement plan had fallen apart quickly. Bree had expected Enzo to throw in the towel right after she retired from Alex Bay High School the year before last. But when Enzo told her how the bank had begged him to stay, how they couldn't function without him, she had relented. She had assumed that he meant he would continue working only a few months longer, at most. It wasn't until two years later that she realized their planned overseas trips through the Alps and down on the Rhine were on indefinite hold.

Bree reached into her pocket and set two pills next to her drink. With a quick swipe, swirl, and swallow, the pills were in her stomach. She snapped open *The River Gazette* to re-read Opal's article, but her smile faded when her eyes landed on two tragically familiar faces at the bottom of the front-page fold – Brian Annetti and Patty Flanagan. *How could they still be missing?*

As the pills relaxed Bree's muscles, the rhythmic grumbles and clanks from a construction site on Sisson Street dampened her senses. Perched high on her deck, she watched a rotating cement truck pull away from the yellow warning tape that blocked the staircase of the once-glorious Thousand Island House. While half of the building's structure remained its decrepit, defunct self, the other half had been renovated and had opened for business under a new name – The Bijou House – and had received top reviews in the first few months of opening. Its prime location on the river's shore and its bragging rights for once housing Daniel Carnegie and Ulysses S. Grant, gave the setting an ambiance of significance with which few competitors could compete. From her vantage point, Bree could see the hotel's original faded, forlorn sign propped against a stack of lumber in the yard, its letters still readable: *Thousand Islands House, Established 1899.*

The past, she thought. *I want to go back.*

The Kennedys had been river regulars with the Schatzes on warm summer nights. While the women typically sipped wine in the bow, the men managed the directions and throttle at the control dashboard.

Although the two were about the same height, Daniel stood straighter than Enzo, making him more dignified than his friend's slightly hunched frame. Daniel captained the trips, steering clear of joyriders and buoys, staying ever mindful of the unpredictability of the river's current.

"I'm more careful now," Daniel said to his friend. "After those kids disappeared, couldn't help scanning the river for their bodies."

Enzo shook his head. "Such a shame."

It was during after-dinner trips upriver that Daniel and Enzo would prognosticate on the current or upcoming seasons of sports teams within a hundred-and fifty-mile radius of Alex Bay.

"What's your take on the Buffalo Bills this year?" Enzo asked.

Daniel held his hand to his head. "I predict 2008 will be a repeat of last year. No playoffs. No Super Bowls in the foreseeable future."

"Why is that?" Enzo said, taking a swig of his beer.

"They can't even choose a quarterback. How are they going to win a Super Bowl?" Daniel said. "I'll tell you what else you don't want to hear: even the Blue Jays have no chance of making the playoffs this year. Hell, I'm already looking ahead to the fall. I have high hopes for the Syracuse Orange."

"We should make a day of it. I haven't been to a basketball game at the dome in ages."

"You stay in that area quite a bit," Daniel said.

Enzo nodded. "I don't like being away from home so often, but the bank needs me." He raised his bottle, clinking it with Daniel's.

By the time they floated under the long turquoise bridge by Wellesley Island, Opal and Bree's merlot consumption had kicked in, and they found themselves traveling recklessly down memory lane.

"You looked like a turnip," Bree said.

"You're one to talk, your prom dress made you look like a blueberry," Opal said.

The two dissolved into tipsy bits of laughter as Bree refilled her glass. "And remember the time I was suspended in sixth grade for defending you?"

Opal formed her hand into a fist. "That Fiona Wilder. She kept asking me why I hadn't wiped the red paint off my face after art class. I didn't start crying until she pointed at me and laughed."

"And that's when I decked her." Bree raised her hand to slap a high-five with her bestie.

Opal recalled the details. "It was when Mrs. Dyan tried to haul you away to the office that Claudine and Ellie came to our defense. They explained everything. She listened to them, and Fiona missed field day."

"No one messed with you after that," Bree said, topping off Opal's glass.

"That was the day I went from being an outcasted freak to a sixth grade badass with friends. That was the day I felt my birthmark become invisible."

Bree extended her arms to pull Opal into a hug but wobbled her hand, sending her merlot splashing over the glass rim and onto the deck. As waves rocked the vessel, the maroon drops elongated into long meandering lines. When they dripped off the hull's edge, they looked like drops of rich, red blood.

CHAPTER 13

The last of the sun's rays had dipped below the horizon when Enzo Kennedy stepped onto his back deck. From the bouquet of yellow and white blooms, he pulled out a yellow carnation and ran it down his sleeping wife's arm.

Bree stirred and opened her eyes. "I must have dozed off."

"It's after eight. Forgive me." Enzo held out the bouquet.

Bree smiled. "What is the occasion?"

"I just wanted to do something special for you today," Enzo said, looking first at his wife and then out at Quill Castle.

Bree took the flowers, inhaling their scent. "You are truly the sweetest man alive. People have no idea." When she set the arrangement on the table, she saw the newspaper beside her empty glass. "Can you believe it has been twenty-five years since those kids disappeared? An anniversary newspaper edition will be out this weekend. Heart-breaking. I remember that night like it was yesterday."

Enzo kept his gaze on the castle. "So do I."

"That was the night of the last Board meeting of the school year, the night the high school bell went missing. I got home so late and was exhausted," she said. "My God! When I walked in and found all that blood in the kitchen – on the counter, in the sink – I thought you were dead. It looked like someone had taken a hacksaw to you."

Enzo nodded. "The night I slipped on the dock and cut my hand."

"And will you ever forget that doctor at the hospital, that son of a bitch, Dr. Byong? Lord have mercy, thank God he retired. He said he could not figure out how that kind of fall could have led to that type of gash. 'What did that even matter?' I had asked him. 'Just stitch up my husband!'"

Enzo rubbed the jagged white scar on his right hand. His voice was soft. "It was an accident. I didn't mean to do it."

"Of course, you didn't," Bree said. "And to think you didn't even want to go to the hospital."

CHAPTER 14

Dr. Hyo Byong leaned against the kitchen counter twisting her badge and lanyard between her hands, waiting for the front door to open. She had purposely booked the emergency Board meeting early, well before her first surgery of the day. Her nerves relaxed when Ruby rushed in.

"Do you have any idea how late you are?" Hyo Byong put her hands on her hips. "The meeting starts at nine."

"I know. I know," Ruby said. "Marion Sibber had a vision last night telling her to have Mount Everest tattooed on her right calf. I met her at seven. Just finished Phase I of it now."

Hyo eyed Ruby from head to toe. "I trust you're not wearing that to meet with the Board," she said, noting Ruby's tight white tank top that just met her short shorts. Her long, layered chestnut curls fell across each shoulder and down her back.

In response, Ruby stripped down to her black bra and panties, feeling Hyo's eyes on her.

Ruby liked Hyo watching her. She liked even more that Hyo had given her some closet space and a drawer in the bathroom for her personal items – razor, deodorant, lotion. Ruby turned to reveal her upper back.

Hyo gasped. "Look at that." Hyo dropped her hospital badge and keys onto the counter. "Is that why you went to Syracuse the other day?"

"Yep. Jasper had some cancellations. You like?"

Unlike her mother's splotch on her face, Ruby's port-wine birthmark that had once spread across her upper back had been transformed into art. Hyo's fingers traced a new line of baby turtles crawling along Ruby's shoulder blades that magically morphed into a scattering of red sails on an ocean wave.

"Your skin is a canvas," Hyo whispered. "How on Earth are you forty-five years old? You have the body of a twenty-five-year-old."

Ruby turned. "Hey. I'm on a time crunch right now. You can explore my nooks and crannies later." Ruby walked to the bedroom and returned holding her pressed clothes. She pulled a black pencil skirt off a hanger and slipped into it, zipping it up with her hands behind her back. She grabbed the tailored white blouse and popped it over her head before smoothing it over her slender hips. With the addition of black pumps, Ruby had transformed into a professional.

Hyo stepped back. "My God. You look like a Republican."

"Correction. I look like a *conservative* Republican. And Republicans would be very impressed that I'm working two jobs to pay my mortgage for *Tats and Brews*. If I get the contract with the hospital, I can hire a manager for the *Brews* part and invest my time on the *Tats*."

"You will get the contract," Hyo said.

Ruby kept her voice firm. "I want to get it on my own terms."

They stared in silence until Ruby broke the tension. "It's probably better we arrived separately. I'm going to take five minutes to review my pitch."

Hyo nodded. "Right. Right," Hyo picked up her keys and left, reluctantly leaving her lover.

Ruby exhaled in relief. She needed to maintain her focus, to deliver her proposal with a combination of authority and grace. She went into the bathroom and looked at her reflection in the mirror. She told herself the advice she needed to hear.

"Don't fuck this up."

Ruby pulled her black Audi convertible into an open parking spot on Drawbridge Drive, a side street near Alexandria Bay Hospital. As she tucked her shades into their velvet case, tourists slowed on the sidewalk to consider if the woman with all that wavy brown hair might be a celebrity, not wanting to miss posting a worthy photo on Instagram or Facebook. *Is that Debra Messing? Minnie Driver?* They were smart to do a double take. From Hollywood actors to NHL players, from presidents to prime ministers, the Thousand Islands drew celebrities to its secluded islands for an extended escape from the daily rigmarole of their lives.

Ruby slid out of her car and reached in to grab her portfolio on the passenger seat when she heard the tinny hum of an electric motor grow louder. She knew who it was without looking, whispering a quick prayer: *Jesus, help me not kill this woman.*

Claudine stopped her golf cart at Ruby's shoes. "Heading out to help people vandalize their bodies?"

Ruby turned to her, offering a fake smile. "Fuck off, Aunt Claudine."

An outraged huff escaped Claudine's lips. "You always were a devil child."

Ruby didn't have time to explore her aunt's disappointment in her but could not resist ripping off the bandage that covered her bruised psyche. She tilted her head. "Why?"

Claudine scowled. "Why what?"

Ruby squared her shoulders. "Tell me why you have the constant need to tell me I'm the spawn of the devil. What did I ever do to you?"

Claudine shifted her little vehicle into reverse. "You should be ashamed of yourself."

"Why?" Ruby said, taking a step closer to her aunt. "Since I was a little girl, you have always found a way to insult me, whether it was how I styled my hair or what I chose to wear. Now, you find it acceptable to insult my career. You are sixty-three and I'm forty-five. Think it might be time to bury the hatchet?"

"Your mother is trying…," Claudine said.

Ruby cut her off. "Leave her out of it. This is between you and me." Ruby adjusted her tone, adding a slice of sympathy to her voice. "If this is because you couldn't have children, I *am* sorry."

Again, a gasp escaped Claudine's throat. "You have some nerve."

Claudine fumbled with the ignition key and backed away. Ruby watched her shift into drive and speed down the sidewalk.

A soft voice from behind her made her turn. "Julia Roberts? I'm from Kansas, and I just love you. Would you take a picture with me?"

Ruby turned to the bulky woman wearing a too-tight Jayhawks t-shirt and considered the request. She smiled. "Sure. What the hell." Ruby slid her arm around the woman's robust waist, and just before her fan tapped her phone to capture their broad smiles, Ruby spoke from the heart.

"It feels good to be loved."

CHAPTER 15

Manor Oak Adult Living was a red brick, one-story facility sprawled over two acres directly across the street from the hospital. Empty wheelchairs sat outside its automatic front doors, and rectangular windows displayed the letters S-U-M-M-E-R cut from orange construction paper in a failed attempt to make the facility appear warm and inviting.

Inside a dim administrative office, a man was bent over a corner table, practically motionless, beneath an arm lamp. With his bushy hair, thick eyebrows and wire-rimmed glasses, he looked more like a mad scientist than a health care professional. Howard Schatz held his breath as he inserted the long tweezers into the glass bottle, carefully adhering a tiny American flag to the tip of a miniature Crow's nest made of bamboo. He inhaled only after removing the narrow metal tool. He stood up straight, ignoring the creak from his back, and lifted the glass-enclosed schooner to his face for a closer examination. Howard smiled.

He hadn't had many reasons to smile lately. After willingly taking the recommendation of the facility's Board of Directors to begin delegating his responsibilities due to his upcoming retirement in a year, he realized too late that he had delegated away too much. When he tried to involve himself in dilemmas or offer input into disagreements, he found himself too unaware of the background details to contribute solutions in a meaningful way. He had essentially made himself obsolete.

Today's most important decision he would make was where to display his completed ship.

He first set it near the front of his desk beside his *Administrator of the Year 2002* plaque, then moved it to the top of a file cabinet before deciding on a wooden bookcase under rows of family photos hanging on the wall – Howard and Claudine cutting their wedding cake, Claudine holding a peach pie with a prized blue ribbon pinned to her apron, Howard and Ruby at her college graduation. The last photo in the row showed Daniel, Opal and Howard linked arm-in-arm at the end of a dock; while Daniel looked directly at the camera, Opal and Howard's heads were turned toward each other. Howard reached up and blocked out Daniel with his hand, leaving only Opal and himself gazing into each other's eyes.

Claudine burst in. Howard froze, keeping his hand in place.

She plopped her large sack of a purse onto Howard's desk, rummaging through it without looking up. "I don't know how you can even tolerate being around that niece of yours. You would have thought that Daniel would have served as a good role model in that family. Ruby told me to 'fuck off' right out there in broad daylight."

Claudine unzipped an outer purse pocket. Finding it empty, she returned her attention to the center of the large leather cavern. "And another thing, I do not know how I'm supposed to keep accurate accounting records around here when I am always the last to know the big news, that the family of a Mr. Mosely signed the paperwork to transport him here from Montauk tomorrow morning."

She stopped searching and spoke to herself. "His eighty-fifth birthday is next month. I'll plan a big party. Maybe I can upcharge them for fine linens." She dug her hand in once more, never looking up. "He'll be a resident on the skilled nursing side in the deluxe suite; they must be filthy rich to lock themselves into that pricing contract. They are most certainly trapped at that rate for the duration of his stay."

Claudine held up a ring of keys in victory, then turned and left.

And that is when Howard dropped his hand, turning his eyes to the wooden ship.

"Trapped forever."

CHAPTER 16

The low hum from fluorescent lights was the only sound in the board room filled with four men and two women. The men sat with crossed arms over their chests; the women's hands were folded neatly on the table. No one smiled.

From her seated spot next to Ruby, Hyo Byong began the morning meeting. "Colleagues, I forwarded Ruby Schatz's proposal to you last week. Since no one replied, I thought it fair to assume that there were no objections to the creation of a new Refinement Services Department here at the hospital." She nodded to Ruby, signaling her to begin her presentation.

Ruby smiled and turned to address her small audience. "Thank you for the opportunity," Ruby began. "It's not every day a tattoo artist meets with a Hospital Board." She had hoped for a small laugh or smile of encouragement but received none.

She plowed ahead. "With tattoo art, I can transform a jagged scar into something specific like a butterfly or create something abstract like a mosaic of shapes or colors. I brought my portfolio of photos with me showing how several mastectomy clients redefined and redesigned their surgical scars." She opened a binder and held it out to a mute audience. "I can pass this around if you'd like."

Silence.

"Well, alrighty, then," Hyo said. "It is with great pleasure that I announce full funding for the new Refinement Services Department at this hospital." Ruby closed the binder.

A balding, red-faced doctor slammed his hand on the table. "This is ridiculous. You waltzed into this position on your father's coattails and think we are all going to bow to you. Let me remind you that as Board President, you do not get a vote." He gathered support from his nodding colleagues. "We are a small hospital that can't possibly afford to offer free elective surgery to patients. The insurance companies would laugh us out of town."

"Dr. Smythe, you are correct," Hyo said. "I don't get a vote. But lest I remind you that my father did what none of you seem to do enough of – value women. We have an international opportunity that we are consistently overlooking. As a Board, you *will* approve the creation of this department which will likely put our small hospital on the map."

A loud guffaw from Dr. Smythe didn't stop Hyo. "Yes, for eight months of the year our Alexandria Bay community holds under fifteen hundred residents. But over the remaining four months, we see the traffic of half a million tourists from around the world. You know this. Our small town has the potential to transform itself into an international beacon in cosmetic artistry. Even with the obvious unknowns, we will forge ahead on this uncharted path, together."

Hyo cleared her throat. "Therefore, as a Board, you will approve the creation of a needed service that offers mastectomy patients and all accident victims cosmetic artistry as part of their standard care; you will do so happily and openly."

"You can't make us," the red-faced doctor barked.

Hyo set her fists on the table and leaned forward.

"Let me remind everyone in this room that I have access to your medical notes going back fifty years and have read every document associated with every malpractice suit filed against this hospital," Hyo said. "While there were some doozies, I found potential cases a review board would find quite interesting." The small audience glanced at each other with uncertainty.

Hyo removed her fists from the table and called out toward the door. "Mr. Kennedy!"

Enzo appeared in the doorway and shuffled into the room. He smiled at the board, shifting his weight from side to side. "I have some truly fantastic news. I was informed this morning that Dr. Byung." He looked at Hyo. "Not her," he said, nodding at Hyo. "Her father, Dr. Jin Byong, who you know now oversees medical records at the hospital, has donated one million dollars toward your new Refinement Services department. The account at the bank was finalized yesterday afternoon. We, at the Alexandria Bay National Bank, applaud this Board's commitment and compassion."

Enzo had expected the sound of applause to fill the room, complete with warm accolades of good fortune and congratulatory pats on the back. He was wrong. Silence hung over the room in a deep, thick pall. It took a nod from Hyo to dismiss Enzo into the hall.

Murmurs and groans of defeat left the members slunk back in their chairs.

Hyo advised her board. "Please, to control your excitement."

Ruby spent the afternoon preparing celebratory dinner on *My Gem IV* by transporting sliced filet mignon, grilled asparagus, glass bottles of Malbec and jars of cucumber water to the galley before Hyo arrived for their intimate cruise. She was grateful to her mother for tucking the ignition key under the lifejackets in the bow's storage areas so she could whisk away Hyo after her shift ended.

At sunset, Ruby dropped anchor offshore the Sunken Rock Lighthouse.

"This is delicious," Hyo said. "You didn't have to do this for me."

"I do nice things for those I love," Ruby said, reaching out, setting her hand over Hyo's. "I wouldn't be where I am today without you."

"Well, that's bullshit." Hyo finished the red wine in her glass with a gulp. "Your work is incredible." She pointed at the horizon, rich with reds, purples, oranges, and yellows, swirling its hues across the sky. "You're an artist who changes lives for the better," she said, then reached out to Ruby's face and tucked a loose strand of hair behind her ear.

"The best part was when you called in Mr. Kennedy. You should have seen the look on their faces," Ruby said, leaning in to spread tiny kisses down Hyo's neck.

"That dickhead owes me." Hyo slid her hand under Ruby's shirt, cupping her breast. Rudimentary details of the day dissolved in the magic of the moment.

And then Ruby spoke from her heart. "I'm yours, bitch."

CHAPTER 17

Sitting at her office desk, Opal fiddled with her chrome nameplate. It slipped out of her hand and landed on the floor with a loud clunk.

"You still there?" said a woman's voice.

"Yes. I'm fine, Ebony," Opal said, kicking her identity across the floor. "Just thinking."

Ebony offered assurances. "Your article was just the tip of the iceberg, and the executives here at Butternut Hollow Books want to publish the entire story, everything you have."

Opal grimaced. "I'm having second thoughts. I have hundreds of tidbits about the Quill family and the castle. The real expert is a man named Ash Burton. I interviewed him earlier this week, and he told me about a possible hidden chamber up in the castle's library."

"You just gave me chills."

Opal ran her fingertip over her birthmark. "Listen, Ash is a purist. He loves the magic of Griffin and Faith's love story. This isn't an avenue he would approve of me exploring any more than I already have."

Ebony cleared her throat. "If I may be blunt: Why would the reaction of a man you just met influence your decision on whether to write a book?"

Opal considered the question. "I have to admit, there's part of me that wants to believe the love story is true."

"But you are a journalist."

"I am a journalist."

"And you want to know."

"And I want to know."

"And I'm glad you want to know," Ebony said.

Mac McAllister peeked his head in her doorway. He wore his uniform, the only outfit Opal knew him to own – a white captain's shirt, khaki pants, and tan boat shoes. His white beard was neatly trimmed. He removed his captain's hat and held it in both hands at his belly.

Once Opal spotted him and nodded for him to stay, she wrapped up her conversation with Ebony. "Let's get in touch next week."

"I'll make sure of that."

Opal hung up. "You got my message."

"Came right over."

"You can always call me, you know, like on the phone. Opal went to the delivered boxes in the corner and used her fingernail to try to tear off the corner of a piece of packing tape.

"Had to drop Ellie over at St. Gregory's church instead of St. Elizabeth's since its construction project starts in a few days. Had to get me some new lines for *The Rhineland* at Earl's anyhow. Weren't no trouble at all." He watched Opal struggle to open the tape, so he clicked open his switchblade and sliced the blade down the tape, splitting it into two.

"Turns out I have been signed by a literary agent who wants me to uncover more secrets within Quill Castle."

Upon hearing that news, Mac accidentally slid the blade too far, slicing his fingertip. Blood gushed from the gash. "Damn it!" Mac put the cut in his mouth and sucked it clean.

"Mac!" Opal ran to her desk and rummaged through her desk drawer. "I must have some gauze around here."

"Naw. It's okay. It's just a little notchy." Mac pushed a button on his knife, and the blade retreated inside. He slid it into his pocket and took out a rag to apply direct pressure on the cut. "What type of secrets?"

"Looks like I need to take another look at the castle library."

"That so? Well then, you better start by looking around the gift shop first."

"Why is that?" Opal said.

Mac kept pressure on the cut. "With all the renovations over the last few years, things aren't where they used to be. The original library is now the gift shop, but the books and shelves behind the register are all original. Not sure if that will help."

Opal nodded. "I'll take all the help I can get."

She was grateful for Mac's kindness and for the added convenience of him living in the back wing of Quill Castle on Starr Island. The state of New York had found it more fiscally responsible to house the head groundsman and his wife on the island rather than paying a security company to secure the grounds year-round.

"What time you looking to head over?" Mac asked.

"How about seven?"

He nodded, but then hesitated, scratching his temple. "A storm front is moving in off Lake Ontario. Better spend the night. River will be too choppy for a return trip. I'll tell Ellie to expect your company."

"Thanks, Mac. I'll meet you at seven on the docks."

"Not the docks," he said. "Meet me in the boathouse. It will be raining by then."

Across town, Mac pulled open St. Gregory's heavy, oak door, quickly spotting his wife, Ellie, sitting in a center pew. He could see from the back entranceway that she was still wrapped in the dark-knitted shawl she had put on this morning, despite the humidity accompanying eighty-degree days with no air conditioning. He took in his new surroundings, quickly concluding that this church was at least twice the size of their home parish and much more ornate with its gold and silver painted angels resting in soft clouds along the church's inner dome. Shiny brass inlays outlined each of the twelve apostles on stained-glass windows.

It must have been a clerk or priest who had posted a warm welcome sign for newcomers: *St. Gregory's welcomes the parishioners of St. Elizabeth's while your altar is being altered. Pray with us.*

Ellie McAllister, a pale, frail woman, whose loose silver braids rested on her shoulders, stared at the golden crucifix hanging above the altar. Jesus' head was tilted to the left as though his gaze was cast directly at hers. Tall, white candles burned in glass cylinders on the tabernacle's ivory cloth. The sharp scent of frankincense lingered in the landscape, likely from a morning funeral procession. Around her wrist was wrapped a rosary made of black, oval beads, one of which she held between her thumb and index finger. Her voice was barely audible as she reached the end of reciting her fourth rosary: "As it was in the beginning, is now, and ever shall be, world without end. Amen."

At the sound of her husband's approaching footsteps, she postponed starting the Apostle's Creed, the next of a litany of prayers, and fell silent, dropping her gaze to the floor.

Mac set his hand softly on her shoulder.

"Opal will be joining us tonight. Want to get some dinner in town before the ride back?"

Ellie listened but remained still. "No."

"Ellie."

"I said no."

Mac knew the conversation was over. He kept his voice low. "I'll stop back for you a bit before seven."

Mac noticed her practically indecipherable nod. He genuflected, made the sign of the cross across his torso, and headed back down the center aisle toward the exit.

Ellie tightened the beaded rosary around her wrist and moved her fingers forward to pinch the next bead. She quietly recited a prayer to herself. "Holy Mary, Mother of God, pray for us sinners."

Her shoulders shuddered at the clack of the church door.

CHAPTER 18

Ash Burton sat on a wooden bench outside the Jefferson County Historical Society with a scowl on his face. He had shifted his folder from his left leg to his right leg and then back to his left. The sign on the door stated it opened at 9:00. It was 9:10.

"Mr. Burton?" a woman called.

He looked up at a tall, slender young woman, whose brown hair was highlighted by two turquoise French braids running down each side of her head. She dropped her gym bag and sat beside him on the bench.

"Yes, I'm Ash Burton." She seemed familiar to Ash, but he couldn't place her. He squinted at her face, her hair, but no moment of awareness reached him.

"I'm Rosa Hudson from Manor Oak," she said. "I took care of your wife on the rehab wing after her hip replacement."

Ash's eyes went wide. "Yes. Yes, of course. We were grateful to you, impressed with how you motivated Vivian into doing her exercises and stretches."

"Happy I could help her. Give her my best," Rosa said. "Are you here for the Historical Society? I'm opening now." She stood and unlocked the door.

Ash followed. "You work here?"

"Only on Thursdays. I'm somewhat of a history buff."

Rosa held open the glass door of the red brick former elementary school, and Ash stepped inside. She dropped her bag on a desk in what was likely once the main office, and she slid open the glass panels that separated her from Ash in the lobby.

"Please write your name and the type of information you are looking for," she said, pointing at a registration book. "Once I know that, I can direct you to the correct room."

"Room?" Ash said, looking around randomly.

Rosa nodded to a map taped to the glass divider. "You are here," she said, indicating a red star. If you were looking for agriculture documents since 1850, I'd send you to Room 3 which is right here," she said, tapping a different spot on the map. "But if you wanted old political transcripts from campaigns or debates, I'd send you to Room 9."

Ash nodded. "I'm here for Quill Family history."

"Popular topic," she said, jotting down details on her desk. "I'm making you a visitor's pass for Room 13. When this was a school, that used to be the art room so it's bigger than the others. All we ask is that you *not* return any documents back to the shelves; instead, put them in the bin marked *VIEWED*. One of us will refile them."

"Of course. Yes," Ash said. "Room 13?"

"Down the hall, on the left. But you have to sign in here first," Rosa said, reminding him.

He looked at the next open line on the roster but paused when he read the name had been written on the ledger a month before – *Opal Schatz, Room 13*. He sighed heavily, then signed his name below hers.

Room 13 was a mess. Stacks of files were propped against shelves, jammed in Plexiglas bins, and crammed between ceramic busts of Picasso and DaVinci, who served as glorified bookends. Ash set his folder on a wooden research table and scanned the signs hanging from the ceiling – *Staff, Building & Grounds, Family, Entertaining, Business, Correspondence, Other*. He headed down the *Staff* aisle, reading the labeled tabs on the folders – *House, Maintenance, Transportation* – and started with the *House* files. He carried a stack to the table and got to work.

Ash Burton's enthusiasm hadn't faded an iota during his opening four hours of flipping through file after file, ledger after ledger, in search of what, he didn't exactly know. The hair on the back of his neck didn't stand on end when he read through invoices for building supplies signed by Griffin Quill and furniture purchase orders with Faith Griffin's distinct signature. He didn't gasp when he read a letter from Griffin to Rockefeller outlining his vision for building an express rail from Manhattan to Alex Bay. *Everything is as it should be,* he thought. *No scandal here.*

"Hope you're finding what you need, Mr. Burton," Rosa said, poking her head in the doorway. "Just wanted to let you know that we close at two o'clock today, so you have about an hour."

He nodded. "Thank you."

Ash stood and arched his shoulders to stretch his back muscles. Under the *Entertainment* section, he pulled out a stiff binder labeled *Menus* and perused the lavish, imported ingredients for formal dinners the Quills held at the Thousand Islands House during their extended stays. Ash plucked through them again, not seeing anything worth exploring in further detail.

When he went to slide the file to its original spot, he saw a small, worn portfolio case behind it. He reached in and pulled it out, setting it gently on the counter behind him. Musty dust made him scratch his nose before opening the flap. He slid out about fifty rectangular menus bound in a thick rubber band. Ash freed them from the band's grip and saw that most were duplicates of the one he had seen in the binder. He picked through them, nonetheless.

INAUGURATION DINNER
Honoring New York State Governor
Benjamin Barker Odell, Jr.
January 27, 1900

FIRST COURSE
Julienne Salad or Vermicelli Soup

SECOND COURSE
Broiled Salmon, Turbot in Lobster Sauce, Filet de Soles, Red Mullet, Trout, Lobster Rissoles, Whitebait
ENTREES
Canards a la Rouennaise, Mutton Cutlets, Braised Beef, Spring Chicken, Roast Quarter of Lamb, Tongue
THIRD COURSE
Quails, Roast Duck, Mayonnaise Chicken, Green Peas
DESSERTS
Charlotte Russe, Strawberries, Compote of Cherries, Neapolitan Cakes, Madeira Wine[1]

It was when Ash flipped over the menu to see the next one that he saw the written notes.

> He's planning to stay in Cornwall tomorrow night. His engines arrive on a barge from Montreal. I will meet you at 7.

> *CeCe has a piano recital at 6:30. Can't meet until 8.*

He scanned through his knowledge of the Quills. He knew Cecelia Quill played piano, and he knew Griffin Quill had ordered two turbines from Montreal to bring electricity to Starr Island to speed up construction. He recognized one set of handwriting as

---

[1] Winston, Sydnee C. "Extreme Dining in the Gilded Age." *National Women's History Museum*, 14 June 2013. www.womenshistory.org/articles/extreme-dining-gilded-age.

matching Faith's signature on the furniture invoices. Ash blinked. He flipped over another menu and saw another private note with the same two writing styles. He flipped another. And another.

Panic seized him when he thought of Opal's name in the registration book, knowing he could not let *that woman* find these. Glancing from side to side, he bundled the menus and tucked them into his leather bag.

He had just closed it when Rosa walked in.

"Time's up!"

"Yes," Ash said with a hint of alarm. "I'll be on my way."

"Sorry to have startled you," Rosa said.

"No worries," he mumbled, breezing passed her into the corridor. He did not slow his pace, not even when Rosa called after him to give her best to Vivian. He simply raised his arm and waved his hand in the air, never looking back.

CHAPTER 19

A feisty rendition of *"Let Us Build a City of God"* clamored out from St. Gregory's steeple, the universal signal to locals that the dinner rush had begun. From her desk, Opal could smell the sweet and salty scent of freshly popped kettle corn seeping its way into *The River Gazette's* office. Opal breathed it in, knowing that the evening festivities at the park must be in full swing.

She exhaled while clicking on the final edition of tomorrow's edition, zipping the digital copy of the twenty-fifth-anniversary edition of the missing teens, to the printers.

Time to power down, she thought. *Finally.*

At the push of the power button, the computer hum faded to silence, filling her with a new, much-appreciated sense of calmness. She clicked off her desk lamp and felt content that she still had plenty of time to grab some dinner and stop home to pack a small bag for her overnight stay at the castle.

Roxie burst through the doorway, breathless.

"What happened?" Opal said, startled.

Roxie held out a glossy flyer that resembled a political candidate's shiny postcard listing campaign promises that, if elected, would likely never come to fruition. She pronounced each of her words with pointed emphasis. "This was delivered to every mailbox in our readership area this afternoon." She handed it to her boss.

Opal's eyes were immediately drawn to the lower right corner and onto a photograph of Claudine, arms folded across her chest, a scowl on her face. "What is this?" Opal answered her question when she read its headline.

> Cancel your subscription to *The River Gazette*.
> Don't let the chief editor's lies destroy
> your family, your lives, your legacy.

She squinted at Claudine's photo. "So that is what you've been up to. Son of a bitch." A bitter laugh escaped her throat as the police chief stepped inside.

"Hollis," Opal and Roxie said in unison.

"Good evening, ladies." He wore the official summer uniform of navy shorts, sneakers, and a white polo shirt, which sported the Alex Bay Police Department logo on its right breast pocket. His shoulder harness held an intercom button that connected directly to central dispatch, while his belt held his holster and gun.

"Is everything ok?" Opal asked.

Hollis did not look comfortable. He bit his upper lip and nodded at Roxie before focusing on Opal. "Claudine has filed a restraining order against you." He held up a folded white paper. "I need you to stay away from her until this is all settled. Judge Branson is due back into town in a few days." He stepped forward, handing the written order to Opal.

A laugh escaped her lips. "Tell me you're kidding." Opal snatched the order from his hand and read it. "I can't believe Judge Branson okayed this."

"His daughter is about to deliver his first grandchild in Pittsburgh. He would have approved anything."

"I want to dispute this," Opal said. "I should have the chance to defend myself, to tell him that my sister-in-law is crazier than a loon."

"You can do that next week when he is back in town," Hollis said, putting his hands on his hips. "But for now, you will stay away from your sister-in-law. No calls. No visits. No contact. Understand?"

Opal saluted the police chief. "Yes, sir."

"Opal," Hollis said. "This is no joke. We'll get it cleared up soon."

"I understand." Opal turned off her desk light. "I have already committed to doing some research tonight at the castle. Mac is taking me over for the night. I assure you I will not have time to worry about Claudine Schatz." She walked to the front door and pushed it open. "Have a good night," she said, waving and smiling at Roxie and Hollis before stepping out the door.

Hollis looked at Roxie. "You believe her?"

"Not for a second."

CHAPTER 20

A homemade peach pie with a glistening golden crust sat on a blue and white checkered placemat at the center of Claudine's gray kitchen island. Across from it were two restaurant-quality industrial stoves beside a double-wide, stainless-steel refrigerator, items she deemed necessary since winning her first blue ribbon in Watertown, NY, at the local Jefferson County Fair. Her logic was clear: to be the best, she needed the best.

Always held the third week in July, the fair drew young and old alike to enjoy sinful, high-caloric sugary sweets, from pink cotton candy spun into portable beehives on a stick to toasted slabs of fried dough doused in powdered sugar. The *'There is Something for Everyone in Jefferson'* theme proved effective, drawing visitors from neighboring counties to tour its livestock barns and even throw a few bouncy orange balls toward a grid, hoping to call out, "*I got it!*"

Claudine attended the fair each of its seven days. She had never bought tickets to ride the Tilt-a-Whirl, the Ferris Wheel, or The Scrambler, the most popular rides on the Fair's main drag. She had never once thrown a dart to burst a balloon that would have sent her home with a giant brown bear or stuffed pink flamingo. Claudine spent all her time each year in Grange Hall, where antiques, quilts, button collections, photographs, and home-baked goods were judged. And Claudine was interested in just one category – fruit pies.

Above her kitchen island hung a cast iron pot rack with no pots. Instead, it served as Claudine's trophy case, her blue ribbons proudly and prominently displayed on black hooks. Before Opal's articles had run in the newspaper, the only two things she had been prouder of than the Fair ribbons were buying the Celtic dagger and being a Quill family heir. As she watched orange flames shoot out from under two tall silver canning pots on the stove, she thought of how Opal had robbed her of what she loved most.

Claudine set a small yellow box beside thirty quart-sized, peach-filled canning jars lined on the counter beside the stove, twenty-nine of which were sealed with gold lids held on by tightened rings. Just one jar of peaches remained unsealed. She hummed a simple tune while opening the box labeled *Arsenic*. And as she had done with the pie, Claudine stuck a spoon into the box and scooped out a heaping pile of white powder, its almond scent rich and bitter. She sprinkled it on top of the peaches in the unsealed jar, careful not to spill any powder. She inserted the spoon into the jar and stirred until the powder dissolved, then carefully set a black lid on the poisoned fruit and tightened it with the last remaining golden ring.

It was then Claudine Schatz did something she rarely did. Smile.

CHAPTER 21

When the pounding began on her front door, Claudine slid the box of poison between boxes of cereal on a shelf. Back at the stove, she used long metal tongs to lower the sealed jars of fruit, one by one, into the hot pots.

Right on time, she thought.

Opal stomped into the room. "You told people to cancel their newspaper subscriptions and filed a restraining order against me? Have you lost your fucking mind?"

"I was just making something for you," Claudine said, never looking up. Like a worker on an assembly line, she finished the canning process by watching the black-lidded jar disappear beneath the rapid bubbles. Her voice was monotone and direct. "You have no right to interfere with people's lives just because you feel like it."

Opal laughed in disgust. "No one knew the dagger had been stolen a century ago. You know this. Mitch was just writing an article about an unusual research project by a college kid in Daniel's class. And I did not publish those DNA results to intentionally hurt you. I was just trying to bring some truth to this town."

Claudine slammed the metal lid on the pot, spinning around to face Opal.

"You like that word *just,* don't you? And I'll tell you why. Because it excuses you, absolves you from all responsibility. You think your actions have no consequences." She locked eyes with Opal. "My God, you have not changed a bit since high school."

"High school was forty-five years ago," Opal said."

"Even with that thing on your face, you somehow always found a way to one-up me. You ran against me for class president and won. You were nominated for prom queen at the last minute, and I bet you still have the crown." Claudine clutched a fist to her chest.

Opal snorted a laugh. "Claudine. We were kids."

Claudine shook her head slightly, making some sort of decision. "No. You took something from me so I will take something from you." She dried her hands on her apron, grinning. "Do you remember once receiving a letter in your locker near the end of senior year?"

Her words rattled Opal, who felt her hands go ice cold. A stream of adrenaline inched up her spine. She could only whisper her response. "A letter."

"You must remember. It was a letter from Howard asking you to meet him down at the dock."

Opal blushed.

***

An eighteen-year-old Opal turned her locker dial left, right, and left again in a crowded hallway. She wore a fringed vest, bell-bottom jeans, and clogs. Random braids were loosely pinned back within her lengthy, auburn hair.

When she pulled the metal door open, a letter fell to the ground. The envelope showed her name: My Dearest Opal. She glanced to the side and picked it up. She leaned into her locker for privacy, then opened and read the letter. Opal smiled, tucked it in her notebook and hugged it close.

***

Opal blinked. "How do you know about the letter?"

Steam swirled from the boiling pots behind Claudine. "Because I am the one who put it there."

Opal shook her head. *That makes no sense*, she thought. "I was already dating Daniel at the time. Why would you give me a letter from your fiancé asking me to meet him late at night at the docks?"

"Because 'My Dearest Opal,' Howard didn't write the letter." A sinister smile spread across Claudine's face, and she set her chin high in victory. "I did."

Opal grabbed the counter to steady herself. "I don't understand."

"We were two best friends in love with two brothers. Howard was mine. Daniel was yours. Plain and simple. I put the letter there as a test."

"A test of what?"

"Your loyalty." Claudine grinned in delight. "I remember watching you leave the musical cast party that night to meet a man who I knew wouldn't be there. That was my victory, picturing you waiting there alone in the rain. It must have been humiliating."

***

A lit cupola atop the boathouse cast its light on the river docks below. The teenage Opal stood in the doorway of the barn-like structure wearing a white, short dress. She looked out the doorway and up at the sky.

***

Opal knew she should turn on her heel and walk out the door, but she felt something click within herself, a movement she knew could not be undone. She exhaled the air in her lungs and slowed her breath before locking her eyes on Claudine.

"I answered the letter." Opal was surprised by her own words, words that she had never spoken to anyone. She repeated her sentence by annunciating each word clearly. "I answered the letter."

Claudine stopped drying the jars. "You did no such thing."

Opal knew there was no turning back now. She had put into motion a course, a track, from which she could not retreat. "I did. I wrote him back saying to meet me at the boathouse instead of the dock because of the rain."

Claudine lowered her eyebrows. "But Howard would have told me."

Opal cocked her head. "Why? He never knew about your letter. Only about my reply."

A brutal silence fell between them until Claudine broke the tension by speaking before thinking: "But why would Howard meet you at the boathouse so late when he was already engaged to me?"

Her own words poked fatal holes in her inflated hubris. Claudine knew, everyone knew, why people met in the darkness of the boathouse. She shook her head. "No. Don't steal this from me, too. Not my Howard."

Opal leaned in close to Claudine's face. "He was never *just* your Howard."

Claudine pushed Opal away, waving her arms between them. "Just like your great-grandmother, you're nothing more than a cheap whore. I've had a lifetime with him; you had him for one night."

But Opal didn't waver. "He gave me more than that, Claudine. He gave me my legacy."

***

A young Opal shifted her eyes from the rain to a young man walking toward her. A freckled, teenage Howard smiled at her. Together, they disappeared into the darkness of the boathouse.

***

Claudine shook her head in denial, her chest heaving with every breath. "No! Stop."

But Opal could not stop. She leaned in again and whispered in Claudine's ear. "Howard. Just. Loved. That. Ruby." Opal turned on her heel and left the kitchen.

The slam of the front door made Claudine flinch. And amid her cooling peach-stuffed jars, Claudine stood alone beside the stove's flames. The boiling water and whistling steam did little to muffle her scream.

CHAPTER 22

By the time the church bells chimed at five o'clock, Opal was yanking the letter out of the top drawer of her bedroom bureau. She peered at its words, searching for a hint, for some subtle clue, that it was Claudine's hand that had penned the note and not Howard's. She wondered which word should have raised a red flag.

My Dearest Opal,
Please keep this letter secret. Meet me at 11 tonight at the docks.
Wait for me there.
Yours, Howard

"She has to be lying," Opal told the decades-old note. That damned letter had fanned her embers of shame into pernicious flames each and every day of her marriage to Daniel. She kept it not for sentimental value and not as a keepsake from Howard; no, she kept it as a reminder of her crime against the man she loved.

Fishing for her phone, Opal dialed Howard's number and waited. No answer. She typed him a text and sent it.

Opal stuffed the letter and her phone into the side pocket of a quilted travel bag. In its center, she packed a nightgown, robe and slippers, her brown notebook, and a change of clothes for the morning. She closed the zipper thinking of her agreement to meet Mac at the docks in an hour. *Would Howard get her message? Would she have time to tell him in person that their secret was out?*

The YMCA's decision to remodel and expand its gym had proved successful. Three additional treadmills and a new line of stationary bikes drew the aging community through its doors during the winter months. It maintained those new members throughout the summer only after they had completed the last upgrade – air conditioning.

Wearing only a towel, a freshly showered Howard opened his gym locker door and checked his phone for any texts from Manor Oak. He saw that he had a missed call and a new text message from Opal. He tapped the notification and read her text.

Claudine knows.
Meet me at the boathouse now.

Howard's knees quickly bent, collapsing him onto the wooden bench with a soft thud; his eyes flashed up to God. He winced in physical pain, shaking his head in disbelief. He texted back, dressed, and left for the boathouse.

Howard arrived first, pacing the planked wooden floor between covered personal watercrafts and speedboats. With his untucked shirt and damp hair, he looked like a wild man.

When Opal appeared in the doorway wearing a raincoat and carrying her overnight bag, Howard went to her, his voice riveted in despair. "Why did you tell Claudine? We had agreed."

"Claudine took something from me, so I took something from her."

"That's something a fifth grader would say."

"It's not. It is simply an eye for an eye."

"And what about me?" Howard said.

"What about you?"

Howard let her go. "Jesus! My wife knows I'm much more than Ruby's uncle. She knows we lied. That I lied." Howard pointed at her. "You don't lose anything from this revelation."

Opal's tone turned bitter. "I have already lost Daniel, and now I will probably lose Ruby when she finds out the man she thought was her father … isn't. How easy will that be to forgive?"

Howard rubbed his forehead, trying to think of a solution. But then he laughed to himself, his voice turning soft. "After Daniel died, I hoped we would start making a plan."

Opal blinked. "A plan for what?"

Hurt filled his eyes. His response was swift. "A plan for us."

Opal contemplated his words. "There is no us."

He stepped forward. "I always thought *we* might have a chance one day."

"What are you saying?" she said.

Howard whispered. "I was going to call it off with Claudine, break our engagement, but then she found the ring I had bought you and assumed it was hers. By noon, the whole town knew. By dinner, she had picked out our China pattern. You were already dating my brother." Tears rimmed his eyes. "You left with him to the army base. You left me here. With her."

Opal secured her bag's strap to her shoulder. "Listen closely, Howard. There was never a chance for us because I did what I never thought I would do. I fell in love with Daniel." Her eyes glistened. "I loved him, Howard. There's no erasing that. Don't go Gatsby on me right now. You should never have made me your green light. I never asked for that; I never promised you that."

Even though Howard heard her words, Opal could still see that the rays of hope in his eyes had not dimmed.

Opal presented him the missing piece of the puzzle. "There's something you don't know. For all these years, I had thought you had written me a letter asking me to meet you here that night."

Howard frowned in confusion. "You're the one who wrote me the letter."

Opal reached into her bag and handed him the worn envelope. "Open it."

Obeying her, his eyes scanned the words. He ran his finger across his signed name and looked at her. "I never wrote this."

She grinned. "I wish I had known that fact forty-five years and one hour ago. Claudine wrote it to make me look like a fool."

Howard gasped. "Claudine wrote this?"

Opal nodded.

"And you thought it was from me," Howard said, his voice ringing hollow. "So, you never asked me to meet here on your own. You never wanted me."

Opal shook her head. "I sent you a note saying to meet here because of the rain. And as you know, one thing led to another." She looked up at the boathouse ceiling. "And here we are again, where it all began."

Their pasts now changed, they stared at the letter that was supposed to harm and humiliate thinking how their lives would have changed had they known the truth. But their angst evaporated when the same thought seeped into their minds simultaneously.

Without the letter, there would be no Ruby.

Panic rose within him. "Claudine will tell her. I'm sure of it."

His words released a stream of tears down Opal's cheeks. "I have to tell her first."

"No," Howard said, stepping in close to her. "Let it be me. Please, Opal. She shouldn't hate you. Let her hate me for this."

Opal heard *The Rhineland's* horn blast a block away. "Mac was supposed to take me to the castle in a few minutes, but I'll cancel. I can't go now."

"Yes, you can. Go," Howard said. "She will need you to help her through this mess."

Opal nodded her agreement. "You will have a day to figure out how to tell her," Opal said. "She texted me that she is leaving for Syracuse later and won't be back until tomorrow night." Opal watched him release a sigh of relief.

A clap of thunder rumbled in the evening sky. They both looked up at the threatening gray clouds.

It was Opal who predicted the future. "Bad storm coming."

CHAPTER 23

On a rolling corkboard he had dragged up from the basement, Ash Burton had pinned up seven stolen dinner menus with writing on the back, each one printed on a varying shade of white linen paper -- ivory, ecru, dove, cloud, lace, alabaster, cotton. The pinned evidence resembled that of a crime scene investigator. After setting them in chronological order, he had written the name and date of each dinner on blue sticky notes to establish a clear timeline.

"You've made progress," Vivian said, walking into the room.

Ash nodded. "Their notes would have been easy to miss." He slapped his hands together in delight. "They communicated during formal events and dinners at The Thousand Islands House."

Vivian couldn't hold in her smile – her sad, sullen husband had transformed himself into a giddy investigator. "Who is 'they?'" she asked.

Ash's eyes were bright. "Faith Quill," he began. "And her lover."

Vivian stood before the board and read the handwritten notes.

January 27, 1901 – Governor's dinner

> He's planning to stay in Cornwall tonight. His engines arrive on a barge from Montreal. I will meet you at 7.
>
> *CeCe has piano recital at 6. Can't meet until 8.*

June 3, 1901 – Industrialists Dinner

> *Ivy trellis by the restaurant. Sunday. Look for my pearls.*
>
> Moved in quilts and pillows to the bungalow.
>
> *Our hideaway.*

November 25, 1901 – Women's League Dinner

> *The boathouse at dusk.*
>
> At dusk. E.

May 3, 1902 – Carnegie Dinner

> *Marble planter in the Rose Garden. Sunday. Look for my ruby bracelet.*
>
> Saw you at breakfast. You are glowing.
>
> *Baby will be here soon.*

July 4, 1902 – Railroad Dinner

> *The boys overheard Doc at the bar last week. Dark hair. He said he had never seen a Quill with so much dark hair.*
>
> *She will be raised a Quill.*
>
> *I want to see her.*
>
> *10:00. Bring the morning train packages to the nursery.*

October 17, 1902 – Fall Harvest Dinner

> *You are joking! F.*
>
> *I cannot stay knowing you continue to share a bed with him. It's too much to bear, watching Pearl grow up, not being able to hold her, teach her.*
>
> *I promise we will find a way. You will have the secret room ready at the castle soon.*
>
> *No. I cannot spend my days watching him, helping him, build a monument of his love for you. HIS love, not mine.*

Vivian read the last line aloud. "His love, not mine."

Ash nodded. "Opal Schatz was right – Faith Quill was having an affair. We know she had a daughter named Cecelia, and I matched the handwriting to furniture invoices she had signed when renovating the Thousand Islands House's dining room, the space they regularly used to host their dinners.

"Who is E?"

"I'm going through staff ledgers and compiling a list of possibilities."

"Are you going to tell the editor what you've discovered?"

He let out a long sigh. "If I don't figure out the identity of E, there is no news to tell."

CHAPTER 24

As dark clouds moved in from the west, tourists gave up their dinner plans on restaurant patios opting for pizza and chicken wings in their hotel rooms. Jagged flashes of lightning lit the sky in the distance.

Claudine sat alone in her kitchen. The poisoned pie and jar of peaches sat in the center of the table under her row of victory ribbons. She knew the trade-off: by setting her plan into motion, she would be committing herself to its outcomes and consequences. She longed for a last intake of inspiration.

Beside her was the bookshelf Howard had made her as an anniversary gift. The twenty-ninth anniversary was supposed to involve new furniture and she had expected a remodeled living room or an expansive front porch.

"It's nice," she had told him before adding, "Is that it?"

She remembered how his smile had faded in disappointment, but she did not care; she had had to stand firm despite his supposedly sincere efforts. She was always thinking ahead – the gift for the thirtieth anniversary was pearls and she didn't want to end up being taken out for a clambake and a large soda.

She had spent years filling his gift's shelves with her favorite works of literature and poetry, including her two prized anthologies. The first was William Faulkner's best works – *A Rose for Emily, As I Lay Dying, The Sound and The Fury*. The second anthology contained only ironic tragedies – *Hamlet, Ethan Frome, Roman Fever* – which she had regularly annotated and dog-eared to mark her favorite lines and likings. Looking up at her peach treats on the table, she knew that Faulkner's Emily Grierson, from her own Jefferson County, would be proud. And that was enough.

Claudine printed her message for her sister-in-law on a white label. With a combination of instilled habit and engrained hubris, Claudine fastened the sticker to the poisoned jar, smirking with satisfaction. She copied the same sentiments onto a second label and attached it to the foil-covered pie. Her message was simple.

For Opal
From Claudine's Kitchen
BEST SERVED COLD

CHAPTER 25

Claudine had recovered from Opal's revelation by the time she stood in front of *Tats and Brews*. She listened to the church bells chime their hymns at six o'clock, creating a cacophony of random clatter rather than a soothing, harmonic tune. She clutched the brown canvas bag that held her peach specialties. Thunder rumbled across the cloudy sky as she pushed open the door.

A jingling bell announced Claudine's arrival. Cradling the bag, she maintained a smug smile as she browsed the photos on the wall, each highlighting Ruby's artistic ability. Claudine looked at her niece, grateful she never had to be a stepmother to the bastard child her husband had produced with Opal. She thought how it was better to never have been a mother at all than to have been a mother to that wicked girl.

Ruby didn't notice Claudine. She was entirely focused on keeping her hands and head close to the belly of a brunette in her late twenties. The high-pitched buzzing from a hand-held machine paused momentarily, just long enough for Ruby to call out, "I'll be right with you," without looking back at the door. The buzzing continued for another minute before Ruby sat back and watched the woman inspect her lower abdomen.

Claudine couldn't hold in an audible "tsk, tsk, tsk," a sound Ruby recognized. She whipped her head toward the door. "Aunt Claudine."

Her aunt waved her off, flitting her hands in the air. "Don't let me stop you. Carry on, there, sweetie."

Ruby nodded pensively and turned her attention back to her client, who had reached out and pulled Ruby close into a tight hug.

"Thank you, Ruby," she said. Sudden uncontrolled sobs gushed from her lips during their embrace. Ruby waited until her wave of emotion weakened and her client's arms relaxed, before releasing her.

"I texted you the follow-up care," Ruby said. "Call if you have any questions."

Her client looked down at the new red heart outlined in black below her navel. "It's perfect."

They met at the register, and after completing the transaction, the woman took Ruby's hands into both of hers. She whispered something into her ear and left.

Claudine watched the young woman leave then turned to Ruby. "My, my. Your client certainly looked like she was in considerable pain. Do you regularly reduce your clients to tears?"

Ruby removed her thin surgical gloves with a snap at the sink, then soaped and rinsed her hands under hot water. "She was in considerable *mental* pain but might start healing now."

Claudine cocked her head, not understanding her comment.

"She miscarried last month," Ruby clarified. "The heart on her abdomen will give her peace, saying the baby was real, saying she will never forget."

Claudine shifted her weight from side to side, not wanting to admit that Ruby could be a compassionate, talented artist. To maintain her focus, Claudine held up the bag and handed it to her niece. "I made these, especially for your mother. It's the same recipe I made for your father."

Hell hath frozen over, Ruby thought, taking the items out of the bag. She set the foil-covered peach pie on the counter and the glass jar of peaches, with the black lid, beside it. She heard herself saying phrases that she didn't typically associate with her aunt. "Thank you. That was nice of you."

"I want to apologize for being short with you earlier." Claudine pronounced her words just as she had practiced on the way over. "You are my niece. I love you."

Ruby nodded. "I will give these to Mom tomorrow night when I get back into town."

Claudine frowned. "Tomorrow?"

Ruby looked at her watch. "I have an appointment tonight in Syracuse at eight and have to head out now, actually."

Claudine didn't move. This was not her plan. Her anticipated images of Opal rotting from the inside out would have to wait.

Ruby gave Claudine a verbal nudge to leave. "It was so sweet of you to make her the peach treats. I'm sure Mom will be in touch."

I'm being dismissed, Claudine thought, never tipping her hand at the wave of disappointment that flooded her mind. She kept her voice upbeat and chipper. "I must be off. I have books to balance and a new resident arriving this evening. Busy, busy, busy." She turned and left, faking confidence in every step.

Once on the sidewalk, Claudine felt hot adrenaline race through her veins. She reviewed her plans for the remainder of the day. She booked a new patient intake at Manor Oak at seven and planned to meet Bree at the church to pack up the altar at eight. This was her open trail of breadcrumbs. If she were ever considered a suspect by investigators later, they could form one conclusion – that Claudine Schatz was nothing more than a dedicated, loyal, God-fearing woman.

The old man didn't mind waiting. At eighty-five, he had already reflected on his life's missed opportunities and woeful regrets. He knew what was next for him. Yet, by the grace of God, his final wish had been granted with his arrival at Manor Oak via a private transport from downstate. He was finally able to sit and gaze out his private bay window at the glorious floating castle that had drawn him here.

As with most beautiful things, the photographs didn't do her justice. He had expected that the gray, ominous clouds would have dampened her presence on Starr Island, but nothing could have been further from the truth. Simply put, Quill Castle radiated light and her pointed turrets created a crisp outline against the sky's tumultuous canvas. He confirmed what he had long heard with his own visual evidence: *she is a beauty.*

He winced as he gingerly slid his arm out of his robe and reached toward his metal tray. With his other hand, he spun the cap off a silver tube of cream and squeezed a glob into his bronzed hand. He strained across his chest and worked a layer of cream onto his shoulder, only far enough to reach the starting point of the mural spread across his back. His vitiligo formed a long, wide row of amoeba-shaped ivory splotches across his shoulder blades that looked like cumulous clouds floating across the dusky sky. His breath was low and deep as he kneaded the salve into his aching muscle.

Voices from the hall made him stop his repetitive motion and slip on his robe, quickly covering his skin's notable design. He rested his head on the cushion of his orthopedic chair and locked his eyes on the castle.

"Welcome to the executive suite, Mr. Xavier," Claudine said in a high-pitched voice. She carried a clipboard filled with thin pink and white forms. She noticed he didn't acknowledge her but maintained his unwavering stare straight ahead.

Claudine continued. "You can call me Miss Claudine. I serve Manor Oak as its accounting manager. I wanted to let you know your account has been paid in full for the next two months. If you need anything, please don't hesitate to contact me. I'll leave my business card with you. My information is listed at the bottom."

He craned his neck up at her.

Claudine held in her gasp at the sight of the white caul covering his drooping eye. She had seen physical deformities in patients before, from surgical scars to amputations, but the sight of his contorted orb felt as though it had some sort of symbolic meaning.

His voice was coarse. "I need paper and a pen." He looked down at his hands.

"If there is a message you would like me to deliver, I would certainly take care of that for you," Claudine said.

"Paper. Pen," the old man said, never lifting his eyes to her.

She clicked her tongue on the roof of her mouth, glancing down at her clipboard. "Of course, Mr. Xavier." She pulled some sheets of paper from under his admittance paperwork and set them on his movable metal tray. She rested her pen on top.

In response, he inhaled deeply and exhaled slowly. "Miss Claudine. That will be all."

Another dismissal.

Claudine straightened the hem of her shirt and tucked her hair behind her ear. She found herself repeating his phrase to him just so she could have the last word.

"Yes, that *will* be all."

CHAPTER 26

Strong winds whipped across the dark blue river under a steady line of steely storm clouds. Mac handled *The Rhineland* well despite its constant rocking between the port and starboard sides of the ferry.

Opal waited on board with Ellie while Mac secured the vessel's ropes to the Starr Island dock.

"Thanks for this, Mac."

"Anything for our hometown celebrity."

Opal simply smiled, not wanting to spoil Mac's ignorance of the bomb that had blown apart her personal life during the last hour. She gripped Ellie's elbow to steady her over the plank bridge connecting the boat to the shore. They stepped onto the dock, passed under a Quill Castle Welcome Center sign, and followed the arrows pointed toward the castle entrance. Mac slid into the driver's seat of a white, four-seat golf cart with a *STAFF* label on its door and started the engine.

Opal helped ease Ellie onto the back seat cushions and crawled onto the seat next to her. She reached over and set her hand on top of Ellie's. "You're so good for going to church every day."

Ellie looked at her. "I go to church every day because I'm not so good."

The first raindrops fell. Mac put pressure on the gas pedal, sending them gliding down the narrow gravel road toward Quill Castle.

Opal followed Mac's directions and found the west wing bedroom for her overnight stay. She stood in the entranceway of the long, high-ceilinged room on the third floor. A tall, cedar chifforobe cast out its balsamic and camphorous scent, instantly relaxing her. She set her bag on the bed's medallion quilt, then ran her hand its intricate star woven into the center and then over its multiple colorful borders. She knew these round-robin quilts were typically crafted by numerous women, each providing her own border. *How many different hands touched this fabric? How many varied cultures are represented in this one blanket?*

A clap of thunder announced that the storm's fury had reached the castle. Wind gusts battered the thin glass windows creating an incessant rattling like a sparrow desperately tapping its beak as a request for safe shelter. She went to the windows and pulled the fabric curtains closed. The lightbulbs in wall sconces flickered twice.

Opal turned with a start to see Ellie shuffle into the bedroom carrying two folded bath towels and a washcloth. "Sorry for the late notice, Ellie. I only need a few hours in the library."

Ellie acknowledged her comment with a soft hum.

Opal swallowed. "Ellie. Talk to me. You do not seem okay."

"I'm just old."

"We're the same age!" Opal said before trying to lighten the mood. "Look. I brought you something."

Opal rustled through her wallet, pulled out a faded photograph, and handed it to Ellie.

Ellie examined it, her eyebrows creasing down, then rising in delight. A soft smile formed as she registered the faded image of four teenage girls – Claudine, Opal, Ellie, and Bree – all wearing graduation gowns and hats and holding diplomas. They stood linked arm in arm beneath a "Home of the Vikings" banner.

"Oh my," Ellie said. "Look at us."

"I found my high school scrapbook while cleaning a closet and it reminded me of how it was back then. We were all such good friends. Now, I hardly ever see you, and Claudine has pegged me as the reincarnation of the Devil. Things were easier back then."

Ellie wasn't listening. Her face softened as she examined the picture. She moved to the fireplace.

"The world was ahead of us back then," Opal said.

Ellie's head snapped up, and when she spoke, her voice was animated and alive. "Wasn't that the year Bobby D'Ruzio released piglets into the high school the night before graduation?"

"It was! The principal wouldn't let the graduation ceremony begin until…"

Ellie raised her finger into the air, then lowered her voice an octave to mimic the man. "Every single piece of swinal evidence is removed from the halls of the high school."

They giggled.

I had forgotten that," said Opal. "He actually said 'swinal.'" They giggled again.

Opal continued down memory lane. "We had such grand plans back then. Didn't we want to go west and get an apartment together? The four of us living under one roof. Could you even imagine?"

Ellie nodded. "That's what most young people want. To dream of visiting far-off places and to follow their wild dreams."

Her voice and spirit faded suddenly, forcing Ellie to grab the mantle to stabilize herself. The photograph slipped from her fingers and cascaded to the floor like the last leaf falling from a tree before winter's arrival.

Opal leaped into action, trying to convince Ellie to sit on the bed, but she resisted and began wringing her hands like Lady Macbeth herself.

Ellie looked into Opal's eyes and whispered her message, her plea. "I want to tell you what happened. I need to tell you. Please."

At the highest moment of Ellie's urgency, Mac stepped into the room, diffusing the intensity. Ellie and Opal's eyes stayed locked on each other until Ellie broke their stare, turning to bury her face into Mac's shoulder. The trio listened to the rain drum against the window.

"The storm is here. I better get you to bed," Mac told Ellie.

Opal picked up the photo from the floor and held it out to Ellie. "Keep this. Here."

Ellie's voice was empty. "No. I don't want it." She curled her hands into her chest.

Gently, Mac put his hand around Ellie's waist. "Come on, now. 'T' bed with you." He nodded to Opal. "You know your way around. Go wherever you'd like. Flashlights are in the library next to the cash register in case we lose electricity. Feel free to take one with you back to your room."

Mac escorted Ellie out.

Opal stared at the photo a moment longer, then tucked it back into her purse. In frustration, she grabbed her brown notebook and headed out the door toward the gift shop, the castle's original library.

CHAPTER 27

The massive crystal chandelier flickered a few times after Opal flipped the switch to light up the enormous room. Scanning the new gift shop from side to side, Opal drew an accurate inference: the transformation from a Gilded Age library to a modern-day gift shop was not a very fluid one. The contrasts were clear – a rumbling Coke machine with a candelabra propped on top, a flickering red and white exit sign beside the painted portrait of Griffin and Faith Quill, and metal hangers perched on the edges of wooden shelves, dangling plush pink, blue and orange *I Love the Thousand Islands* hoodies for visitors.

Opal put her hands on her hips. Her gut told her to ignore the modern enhancements and upgrades, to keep her focus on the bound books hidden behind the sweatshirts. After folding and stacking the clothing intended for tourists on the register, she turned to the books and ran her fingers over the bound volumes, tugging out faded receipts and purchase orders that had been haphazardly tucked between them over the years. She grabbed a few books off the shelves and nestled herself into a sheet-covered wingback chair. She read a chapter about Puritans arriving in Salem, an instructional guide for building Jacobean furniture, and a woman's guide to marriage circa 1810.

    Hours passed. Opal yawned. After a sudden boom of thunder, the light above momentarily dimmed. She got up, returned the books to the shelf, and reached higher to grab another text for inspection. When she pulled it out, she noticed a scalloped-edged photograph tucked next to it on the shelf. She examined the black-and-white image that captured a stately man in a pin-striped suit standing beside a woman in a corseted dress carrying a lacey parasol. They stood in front of a Ferris wheel. A chauffeur stood slightly behind them in his buttoned suit and square hat.

    "Griffin and Faith Quill at the St. Alex Carnival." Opal peered at the servant in the photo. There was no question about it. Invisible to Griffin, Faith's left hand held the servant's right hand. Opal turned the image over and read the handwriting.

                My Everett, 1901

"And who might you be?" Opal asked herself.

    The dim light above flickered again. She tucked the photo into her brown journal, knowing Ebony White would be pleased.

CHAPTER 28

In Mac and Ellie's east wing bedroom, fragile windowpanes let wind slip through their cracks, sending the sheer white curtains floating like convulsing ghosts. Mac snored lightly. Beside him, Ellie stared in terror at the dancing curtains. She burrowed her fists into her eye sockets, trying to expel the events of that day so many years ago.

***

Ellie covered her yellow summer dress with a soft pink floral apron dotted with white daisies. She slipped it over her head and tied its thin strands in a bow behind her back. A white ribbon accented her blond braid. Waiting for the blustery rain to end, she stood barefoot at the sink, running water from the faucet to wash some plates. Steam rose from the hot, soapy water.

She was drying a plate with a dish towel when she first heard the noise. She turned off the water and listened.

"Everything okay?" a voice said.

Startled, Ellie dropped the plate which shattered into sharp shards on the floor. She turned to the doorway. "Enzo! You scared me to death. I knew I heard voices." She peered behind him. "Is someone with you?"

Every stitch of his clothing was wet. From his soggy Polo shirt and plaid shorts to his water-logged boat shoes, Enzo was drenched. He slid out a folder from under his shirt and set it on the table. "I'm so sorry, Ellie. I thought Mac told you I would stop by to check on you while he was out of town."

She thought, then nodded. "You know? He did. He didn't like the idea of my being all alone while he stayed the night in Buffalo for that conference, especially with the storm coming."

"Let me help." Enzo found a broom and started sweeping the glass pieces into a pile.

Ellie would have normally insisted on a guest not sweeping up a mess, but she couldn't take her eyes off the folder he had set on the table. It looked official, so she sat in a chair beside it. "What's that?"

"Unfortunately, I must give Mac some unfortunate news on Monday." Enzo sighed heavily. "I was hoping you could advise me on how to soften the blow."

"Bad news?"

Enzo grimaced convincingly. "His loan was denied."

Ellie swiveled toward him, shocked. "That's ridiculous. There must be some mistake." She opened the folder and flipped through the pages.

Enzo propped the broom against the wall and pulled up a chair next to her. He leaned in close, inhaling her scent, watching as she tried to make sense of intimidating numbers and elaborate graphs.

She turned to him, and Enzo sat back to explain. "The state took over the executorship of Starr Island when the castle restoration project was first approved."

"That's right. In '74, we had just moved out here after our fourth anniversary."

"Both of you took up residence here on Starr Island at that time?" *Enzo said.*

"Yes, that's when he was hired as head groundsman to manage the construction supplies and the day-to-day repairs and maintenance."

Enzo nodded. "The state wants to collect back taxes, claiming this was technically your primary residence."

"Living here was a job requirement," *she said helplessly.* "How much do they want?"

"Eleven thousand dollars."

Ellie jumped from her chair.

"What? We don't have that kind of money. There has been a mistake," *she said, biting a nail.* "This will destroy him. My God. He has been working himself to death to prove himself. No. He can't know about this. There must be a way. Please, Enzo." *She set her hand on his shoulder.*

Enzo ran his hand through his thinning hair. "Well, I could petition the state to reconsider based on the terms of employment when he was hired; maybe I could find a way to make this go away."

Ellie clapped her hands like a cheerleader celebrating a victory for the team. "Do it. Please. I'll do anything,"

Suddenly, Enzo lunged at Ellie, pinning her outstretched arms against the wall. He forced his mouth over hers, muffling her screams with the force of his jaw. He pushed his knee between her legs.

Ellie threw her head from side to side to avoid his mouth but could not break his grip. "No! Stop it!"

Enzo slammed his hand over her mouth and nose with such force that a red river flowed from Ellie's nose and over Enzo's hand. "Don't fight me, Ellie."

Ellie stilled, nodding at Enzo, who loosened his grip on her mouth and began to pull back his hand.

And as a response, Ellie sunk her teeth deep into the soft, fleshy skin between his thumb and index finger on his right hand. Enzo screamed in pain but managed to keep her pinned. Their blood dripped down her chin, seeped into her apron, and splashed onto the floor.

Unable to handle the pain, Enzo released her and wrapped his torn hand in a dishtowel at the sink. Ellie escaped through the doorway leading into the castle.

And that's when Enzo started to laugh. Hard. He called out through the doorway, his voice echoing down the vacant hallways. "I'm leaving, Ellie! With no loan, I'll see to it that you're both evicted by the end of the month."

He picked up the folder and turned to walk out the door but stopped when Ellie appeared in the doorway. She ran at him, grabbing his shirt with her fists. "Who the hell do you think you are? Mac can't know about any of this. My God. Not about the taxes or what happened here. None of it!"

Enzo resumed his attack with sudden swift movements, pinning Ellie to the floor and shoving his hand under her dress. She tried to push him off, to wiggle herself free, but Enzo kept her trapped under his weight.

Darkness filled Ellie's mind; she closed her eyes. She stared blankly at the ceiling, cringing at each of his thrusts as Enzo raped her on the kitchen floor.

Enzo's bloodied hand pulled the white hair ribbon from her braid, its satin fibers absorbing their blood. When he was done, he stood and dropped the ribbon on Ellie's chest.

When Ellie awoke, she was alone, splayed open on the floor amid glass shards and blood. She cried out, rolled onto her side, and vomited stomach bile. Disoriented and unsteady, she used a chair to help herself stand before looking down at the scene. She smoothed her red-stained apron over her dress, then bent down and lifted the bloodied ribbon from the floor, locking it into her fist.

Swaying in the dimming light of day, Ellie stumbled out the door toward the river wanting to wash Enzo's smell from her skin. It was when she steadied her legs and took a step forward that she saw a red canoe resting under the willow. Forcing herself to find her bearings, she stumbled to it, seeing the backpack and gum wrappers.

Her mind raced. Did they see? Will they tell?

"I heard voices," she said, looking back at the castle.

Back in the castle, Ellie grabbed a flashlight and ran through the grand ballroom, up the center staircase and into a bedroom. She crossed a hall into the study, finding no one. Once back in the hall, it was a silver glint that caught her eye. On the floor outside the library's closed door, Ellie picked up a crumpled shiny wrapper that smelled of cinnamon. She opened the door and saw the unlocked bookshelf revealing the secret room.

"What is this?" she whispered.

Ellie inched tentatively closer to the wall of books, flicking on the flashlight whose beam showed her a chair facing the window, a pile of pillows and blankets in a corner, a dressing table, and the jewels. Below her feet, she felt the floorboards shift, seeing the gaping hole in the floor. When she peered into it, she flinched in fright, letting the bloodied ribbon slip from her hand and fall into the crater of darkness. She leaned forward and shined the light down onto two dead teenagers, crumpled and broken at the bottom of the abandoned shaft.

She spoke to the lifeless pair. "I heard you, but then Enzo."

Ellie shook her head from side to side. "No one can ever know. Mac will lose everything."

She examined the jewels in the palm of her hand, before noticing maroon splotches on her apron. She quickly loosened the tied strands and dropped the fabric to the floor at her feet. Turning to flee, she never saw the blood-stained apron slip into the dark chasm. Ellie simply backed out of the room, set her scratched, blood-streaked hands on the secret door, and pulled it closed.

Click.

Ellie then burrowed her fists into her eyes and screamed.

***

Ellie flailed her arms wildly in bed, grunting and groaning in chaotic fear. Mac tried to calm her. The rumblings of the storm's fury echoed down the stone hallways.

Opal rushed in. Ellie leaped off the bed and went to her.

"They're here! They're still here!" Ellie grabbed Opal's shoulders. "They were like us. Maybe they wanted to move to California."

"Who?" Opal said.

Ellie covered her ears with her hands. "I still hear them. I heard them that night."

Opal and Mac exchanged a concerned glance.

"Show us," Opal told Ellie.

Ellie grabbed her wrist and dragged Opal out the bedroom door. Mac followed.

Ellie led the pair into the former library and threw herself against the bookshelves, sending some tumbling to the floor. She grabbed the wooden shelves and tugged on them, desperately trying to yank them open. "It's here! Please help me. Help me find the handle!"

The color drained from Mac's face. "She's never done this before."

"I believe her," Opal said.

Mac nodded in agreement, signaling that he was all in. They joined Ellie and ripped books from the shelves. They helped Ellie search for an answer to an unknown question.

Ellie's hands were frantic. "The door has to be here. I remember. It was right here." Her frustrated cries weakened to soft sobs as she sank hopelessly to the floor.

Mac went to her side, setting his arm across her shoulder. "Ellie. I'm here."

Ellie looked up past Mac's face and gasped. From her new vantage point, she whispered the answer. "I see it." She lurched toward the shelves. "I see a switch. Push hard when I say," Ellie said. She pulled a release lever.

Click.

"Now!" Ellie cried.

All three pushed and the heavy door creaked open.

The ray from Mac's flashlight shook as he frantically scanned the hidden room from side to side, his mind trying to make sense of the scene before him. A guttering moan rolled in his throat when he focused the beam on the dust-ladened, undisturbed room Ellie had last seen twenty-five years ago.

"What the hell is this?" Opal asked.

Mac stepped forward but Ellie grabbed his arm, pulling him back. "Don't fall, love. Down. Down."

Mac moved the light onto the hole. "Jesus. The floorboards collapsed."

Opal and Mac carefully leaned forward as he aimed the flashlight down to the very bottom, illuminating two skeletons wearing faded shirts of vintage rock stars. Blond strands covered one skull's eye socket; a deep crack ran down the other.

Mac swallowed hard. "Jesus, Mary, Joseph." He made the sign of the cross over his chest.

"Brian Annetti and Patty Flanagan. Presumed drowned," Opal said.

Ellie cried tears of relief. "I'm free. I'm finally free."

Mac turned to his wife. "Ellie! How did they get down there?"

She took a deep breath and exhaled excitedly, clasping her hands in front of her chest in pure joy.

"I did it. I locked them in."

PART TWO

June 21, 2015

CHAPTER 29

"You got old."

FBI Agent Benjamin T. Franklin was relieved that Luke Annetti's greeting had been tame. When following up with victims' families in cases he couldn't solve, he had been threatened, chased, ignored, and shot. Ben welcomed the insult, but then fully registered the toll a missing son had taken on the man. The once tall, muscular foreman of a construction crew, a man with broad shoulders whose biting blue eyes somehow commanded immediate attention from anyone he met, now sat hollow and withered. His messy hair, sagging cheeks and crouched frame resembled a man far older than his sixty-seven years, while his simple clothes, blue jeans, dark shirt, thin jacket, work boots, all fell under the category of one word: worn.

Suddenly self-conscious, Ben had the urge to tug together the two sides of his unzipped black jacket, having chosen to keep it open since noticing last year that his zipper struggled a bit when traveling from his waist to his neck. Ten years Luke's junior, Ben had aged more gracefully; his salt-and-pepper hair was still thick, and even though three repetitions of push-ups and pull-ups had left his daily workout years ago, he still ran three miles a day. His eyes did not resemble sapphires like Luke's, but did, in fact, match Crayola's espresso crayon to a T.

Twenty-five years ago, the two men had sat across from each other under a sparkly 'Congratulations Class of 1990' graduation sign in the Annettis' backyard, an area that was supposed to be filled with guests standing in lines to load roast beef, Italian sausage and roasted red potatoes on waxed paper plates. By mid-morning, though, it had been transformed into an FBI command center investigating the disappearance of the boy and his girlfriend. From the buffet table, Ben directed communications between local and federal officers, in direct view of rectangular tagboards covered with color snapshots of Brian Annetti's life – Toddler Brian stuffed into a legit Donatello costume, Young Brian holding a bat in his orange t-ball uniform, Teenage Brian gripping his driver's license behind the wheel of his first car, and High School Brian at the beach with his buddies clutching a football in one hand and holding up a peace sign with the other.

Today, Ben and Luke sat in wicker chairs on the front porch of a weathered cottage overlooking Lake Erie, an orange sunset lighting up the evening sky over Buffalo, New York. They watched a white heron swoop down and scoop up an evening snack from the shallow waters before pounding its wings mightily toward the sky. Ben hoped the quiet would help keep the moment calm. He patted his jeans pocket, glad he had switched his phone to airplane mode to avoid interruptions.

"Heard about your hand back in the day," Luke said, nodding at Ben's titanium wrist and fingers. "And then I saw you on our news for that bomber case here last year, so I knew you weren't dead." Luke scratched his stubbled chin, then tucked his hands into his jacket pockets. "You can't seem to keep yourself out of the limelight."

The embedded insult stung. Since cracking the bomber case, Ben had actively avoided fanfare like the plague. He had learned to pass off press conferences to his superiors and kept himself out in the field as much as possible, be it a campground, fairground, playground, battleground or even underground; he just did not like being in the foreground.

But that is precisely where he had ended up last year when Milo Wurstner, the local lead FBI agent, had broken his leg after slipping down a flight of stairs at the Anchor Bar's annual chicken wing-eating contest. Ben had been the closest investigator available at the time and lost his argument that his current case was more important than the entire population of the city of Buffalo. His job was to find a bomb supposedly hidden by someone calling himself the Freedom Bomber, whose target was Buffalo City Hall on the Fourth of July, a time when thousands of people would gather at Niagara Square to celebrate America's birth by eating and drinking too much.

On his drive into Buffalo that afternoon, Ben had purposely avoided the downtown area, mainly due to the lack of warmth his investigative tactics had received back then. Despite the urgency to find the bomb and the self-proclaimed Freedom Bomber, Ben had started that case like he did all his cases – by selecting a point on the circumference of the crime scene and simply sitting there for a while. It was a strategy that instantly pissed off the rest of the investigative crew who had been working to the grind before his arrival. That day last year, he had chosen a city bench outside of Trinity Episcopal Church and worked swiftly to analyze his surroundings – wind direction, church bells, loading docks, security cameras. It hadn't taken long for the whispers to begin -- *working hard or hardly working, the old man cometh, this guy is for the birds.*

He had ignored the comments, knowing full well he needed to rely on his senses and intuition to catch a raging psychopath who intended to blow up thousands of people. Moments after he had sat down, squawking seagulls and chirping sparrows landed near him, hoping for a stray French fry or corn chip to be thrown their way. Through the years of using this strategy, he had learned that seagulls lost their interest in him rather quickly but that sparrows were persistent little fuckers.

He had once watched a squawking sparrow build its nest with common trash; the winged critter had picked up a garbage twist-tie from a filthy street and added it to support the nest's walls. When Ben examined it closer, he saw a fast-food chicken sandwich wrapper lining the nest's bottom. So when a Buffalo sparrow tried to pick up a piece of string near a pothole for ten minutes straight, incessantly chirping all the while, Ben broke protocol and got up to shoo it away. And that is when he saw the thin wire.

An ignition wire.

It ran out of a manhole cover, across an access road, and into a maintenance shed.

In less than an hour, Buffalo's Bomb Squad, formally known as the Hazardous Devices Unit, found and disarmed a mammoth fertilizer bomb in the shed under a fake planked floor. The bomb was set at the mouth of a tunnel that ran directly to the basement under City Hall. From the time the sparrow irritated Ben to the time the bomb was disarmed, fifty-seven minutes had passed. The Freedom Bomber was later found wearing only his underwear in a nearby motel with twenty-five Molotov cocktails lined up on the bathroom sink.

On his flight back to Albany, Ben proudly thought just one thing: *I guess I am for the birds.*

But that wasn't the end of it. The press had a field day about an FBI agent named Benjamin Franklin with a bionic hand saving downtown Buffalo just days before America's birthday celebration. He declined all national (and international) interviews, personal invitations from municipal bigwigs and all the bribes that came along with those offers. Despite his efforts for privacy, he was unable to stop his face from appearing on every magazine cover and newspaper's front page across the country and around the world. Fans compared his stature to Pierce Bronson and his ruggedness to Kurt Russell. His cover was blown. He couldn't buy a quart of milk or a loaf of bread without inevitably being asked to sign an autograph in frozen food or to snap a selfie with a fan in produce. That's when he called his boss to say he would retire.

The urge to tie up loose ends brought him back to the one case he could not solve.

Luke narrowed his eyes. "I doubt you're here for a social visit."

Shame made Ben break from Luke's stare. He forced himself to refocus, to meet the empty eyes that had haunted him over the last two decades. "I wanted you to hear it from me. Your son's case is being closed since there have been no new developments or leads." Ben waited for Luke to jump up or to unleash a relentless string of profanity, but Luke Annetti didn't move. "And I'm retiring on July first. I will forward all my files directly to the agent assigned to the case. He's a good guy. His name is Pete Murphy."

Luke nodded his head and started rocking his chair back and forth. "But you never found my son. You were never able to find Brian or Patty," he began. "You *did* find the missing twin brothers in 1995, and you certainly found the remains of that little girl in Poughkeepsie in 2001. You found them, but not mine, never mine." He grinned. "If you came back here to tie pretty bows on your failures, Agent Franklin, then you've made a terrible mistake."

In the better light, Ben could now see Luke's worn jeans, stained windbreaker, and unshaven face. "You are not here to tell me about your retirement or about Peter Murphy. You are here to ask my forgiveness. And that is something I will never give you."

Ben stood up. He spoke with confidence and authority. "I'm sorry, Mr. Annetti. I am."

Luke's cheeks went scarlet red. "That's horse shit and you know it."

"Mr. Annetti, it's just that the case hasn't seen any new evidence to warrant keeping it open."

"When the FBI stops following up on tips, how can there be any new evidence?"

Ben frowned. "What tips?"

Luke threw his head back and laughed. It was a hearty, deep laugh, full of both disbelief and spite that quickly transformed into an uncontrolled emphysemic coughing attack. He leaned forward, putting one hand on the porch banister and the other around a corner pillar as he wheezed for air. He managed to see Ben take a step toward him for help but held up his hand to stop him. When his breathing returned to somewhat normal, he wiped his wet eyes and looked at Ben.

"Letters have been delivered to *The River Gazette* for *years* with people claiming to have leads," Luke said. "Opal contacted your office every time something arrived, but your FBI never could find the time to investigate, dismissing her, dismissing *us*, suggesting they were likely sent in by crackpots not worthy of their time."

Ben frowned again. The name Opal sounded familiar, but he could not place her. "This is the first I am hearing of this, Mr. Annetti. I'll let my replacement know. I hear he's good, and I promise you he will follow up on all leads."

Luke spat on the ground at Ben's feet. "That's what your word means to me. I know my son didn't drown and so do you. His canoe was found on land. He made it to Starr Island." He raised his left hand and pointed east toward Quill Castle, two hundred and ten miles away. "I worked for years on that restoration construction crew, and I know that castle better than anyone. He's in there!" Luke returned his hands to his jacket pockets. "You know it, and I know it."

Ben spoke softly, still backing the company line. "With so little evidence found back then – no crime scene, no bodies, no witnesses – it's impossible to justify keeping the case open."

It was then Ben that spotted the gun in Luke's right hand.

"You need a crime scene to keep the investigation open?" Luke asked. "Here you go." And on his last word, he raised the pistol to his head and pulled the trigger.

CHAPTER 30

Luke Annetti was still alive when the ambulance pulled away from the cottage. Emergency vehicles and squad cars cluttered the driveway and front lawn. Ben's goal of fading into the woodwork had again failed.

The undersheriff took Ben's statement, clearing him to leave.

"Do they think he'll pull through?" Ben asked.

"He might. It helps that he used blanks."

"You know that already?"

"If he had used bullets, the coroner would be here."

Ben nodded and turned to the driveway. He almost made it to his car uninterrupted.

"Remember us?" asked a young officer, motioning to his partner. "We drove you to the airport after you found the bomb last year."

Ben nodded. He recalled that he had privately nicknamed them Ren and Stimpy. "That's right. I remember. Rico and Simon, right?"

"Right!" Rico said.

Ben could think of just one phrase: *Please don't ask me for an autograph.*

The memories of last year's media hoopla flooded Ben's senses. Tabloid photographers were relentless in their strategies and attempts to snap photos of the man they dubbed Bionic Bones.

Embarrassing.

His artificial mechanical hand and fingers had kept him interesting and relevant to two segments of society – elementary school kids and needy women; children were convinced he was a robot while women wanted to explore the possibilities of his titanium fingers. Even though Ben had decades of investigative experience, he learned too late that he had been too naïve when answering reporters' questions. In fact, when he was asked why he always wore dark jeans and white t-shirts under his FBI jacket, it had never occurred to him that he was being asked a fashion question. His simple "I like being comfortable" answer electrified his admirers, landing his photo on the cover of GQ.

"Did you give Luke Annetti the news?" Rico asked.

Ben cocked his head. "I came here to tell him his son's case was being closed."

Rico snorted a laugh. "That's obviously not happening now."

Ben blinked. "Why, obviously?"

The two officers exchanged glances.

"Because they found them," Rico said.

"Found who?"

Simon blurted out the answer. "Brian Annetti and Patty Flanagan."

Simon had bad timing. "Do you think I could get a photo of you with that hand on my shoulder?"

Ben ignored the request and took a step closer to Rico. His voice was low. "Explain yourself. Now."

"They found the missing teens in Alex Bay. The news broke right when I turned into the driveway," Rico sputtered. "Luke Annetti just shot himself on the day they found his son."

Airplane mode.

No sooner did Ben change his phone settings with a tap of his finger, than he watched notifications for thirteen missed calls and thirty-four missed texts explode before him.

"Where were they?" Ben said.

"Somewhere in the castle," Rico said. "They arrested someone, too."

"Arrested, for what?"

The young officers spoke in unison. "Murder."

Ben took a few steps back. Luke Annetti had been right all along. Simon figured out quite quickly that there would be no personal photo with the titanium hand when Ben leaned over and vomited onto a patch of yellow daylilies.

CHAPTER 31

Gasoline fumes swirled in a jellied film above the smooth current of the deep swift river. With a waxing crescent moon high in the sky, every law enforcement vehicle that floated was tied to Quill Castle's dock. A Coast Guard cutter bobbed at the front of the line, its red lights flashing.

Opal and Roxie sat on each side of Mac at the kitchen table. Detectives and investigators traveled to and from the castle carrying clear baggies marked with black letters. Some whispered in groups. One woman wore a black jacket with a large yellow label: *Coroner*.

Opal leaned toward Roxie. "What are they saying about the room? Was it a storage area?"

"Looks like a Gilded Age version of a safe room to me. Maybe Griffin had some titillating activities planned for his young wife," Roxie said, raising her eyebrows twice. "Too bad you made the history expert cry. Maybe he would know."

A groan escaped Opal's lips. "I thought of that. No way Ash Burton would give me the time of day even if I begged. Leaning closer to Roxie, she whispered, "I want photos of the crime scene."

Roxie nodded, then slipped out of her seat toward the grand staircase that led up to the third floor. Her mission gave Opal and Mac some privacy.

What Opal wouldn't give to ease Mac's grief. She saw his vacant stare at his folded hands; she watched his shoulders droop forward in despair.

"They're going to indict her," Mac said.

Considering Ellie's confession, Opal knew this was true. "Will Jana represent Ellie?"

Mac straightened his back and kept his voice low. "Yes. Just spoke with her, and she said I should stay here with the police. She's at the boathouse waiting for them to bring Ellie in."

Opal jotted that down in her notebook. "I'm trying to make sense of this. Do you remember anything Ellie told you about their disappearance?"

"I was out of town at a builders' conference that night. I don't know what happened here."

"Did she *say* something happened here?"

"No. Never did. But Ellie had scratch marks on her neck, and her hands were ripped up." Mac slammed the palm of his hand onto the table. "Did those kids attack her? Did she attack them?" His anger faded as quickly as it had arrived before hopelessness settled in. "All I know for sure is that the night those kids disappeared was the night I lost my wife."

Opal set down her pen. She reached across the table and gently squeezed his hand. "I'll be careful how it's written for the paper."

"Appreciate that," he said, nodding. "I can't understand why Ellie kept this from me."

Opal nodded. "Mac, what did she tell the police back then?"

Exasperated, he ran his hands through his hair and told the same story again – that she had waited for Enzo, that she didn't hear or see anything, that she found the canoe in the morning and called the police.

"Enzo Kennedy was here that night?"

"I had asked him to check on Ellie. I thought she might be scared being alone here and all. But he never made it; he ended getting stitches in the ER." He grinned. "It's the only night I haven't slept by my wife's side." Tears glazed his eyes. He buried his face in his hands.

An officer approached him and whispered into Mac's ear. He turned to Opal. "They want me to show them around upstairs." He stood.

Opal couldn't hold back another question. "So, you never saw that room behind the bookcase?"

Mac shook his head. "Lived here forty-one years. Never knew." He turned and followed the officer toward the interior of the castle, passing Roxie heading in the opposite direction.

Roxie returned to her seat. She put her phone on the table and folded her hands neatly, looking smug.

"How did you *possibly* do that so fast?" Opal said.

"After I got Officer Kincaid to tell me all about the size of his gun, he stepped into the hall to speak with the coroner. I took as many as I could. Haven't even seen them yet," she said, handing her phone to Opal. "If there is anything good, I want a raise."

Roxie left to join a few investigators on the lawn, chatting them up for any releasable crime scene details. This gave Opal a chance to scroll through Roxie's photos. Four images were blurry and nondescript, but the other five were clear – two of the gaping hole in the floor, one of two crumpled intertwined skeletons, and one of bedding stacked in a corner beside a makeshift vanity. With a few taps, she sent them to her email.

Opal joined Roxie outside on the lawn. "A raise it is," she said, winking and handing Roxie her phone.

"Are you going to use any of those?" Roxie asked.

"Only the hole in the floor, not their bodies," Opal said. "I'm not running any images of their remains until the parents are notified." She looked at her wrist. "I only have a few hours to change the front-page article and headline. I'll leave my notes on my desk if you need them for your article."

"I'll stay a bit longer and get shots of the cops investigating," Roxie said. "You go."

A sudden thump-thump-thump of a helicopter echoed from above. Opal looked up. "Word's out?"

Roxie nodded. "The morning ferry will be full of every reporter east of the Mississippi."

A whistle from the Coast Guard's boat signaled it was getting ready to leave with Mac on board. Opal rushed down the dock and onto the cutter.

CHAPTER 32

After receiving several assurances from Rico that he would update him every hour on Luke Annetti's condition at the Erie County Medical Center, Agent Ben Franklin generously exceeded the sixty-five-mile-per-hour speed limit on the New York State Thruway. By the time he arrived in Alex Bay, it was just after midnight.

Ben parked at the Alex Bay Marina and walked to the end of a dock to watch the flurry of activity on Starr Island from the shoreline. He rubbed the back of his neck.

I need to get to that crime scene, he thought.

He spotted a teen sitting on the ending planks of a boat dock, smoking. "Hey, there. Is that one yours?" Ben pointed at a blue Jet Ski bobbing in the water.

The teen looked up at him, quickly dropping the blunt into the river.

"Yeah."

"I need to borrow it to get out to that crime scene." He pointed at the swirling, flashing lights surrounding Quill Castle.

"My dad would kill me. No way."

Ben used his titanium hand to hold up a hundred-dollar bill. "What's your name?"

"Henry."

With his other hand, Ben flipped open his FBI badge. "Well, Henry, I have some good news. You get to walk away with a hundred bucks, and I'll be sure to tell your dad that you helped with a federal investigation."

Staring at the cash, Henry reconsidered the request. He shook his head. "I won't let you take it, but I'll drive you out there."

Ben did not expect hardline negotiation from a teenager. "Look, son. I don't think you understand."

"Sir. If I screw up one more thing this month, my dad won't buy me a car," Henry said, clearing his throat before delivering his final ultimatum. "So, you can either climb aboard or find someone else to get you out there."

Ben handed him the hundred bucks.

Henry tucked the cash into his pocket and untied the watercraft from the wooden pier. When the teen reached out to give Ben's elbow extra support, Ben waved him off and straddled the rear seat on his own. Henry slid into the driver's seat to handle the controls.

"What happened out there?" Henry asked, tipping his chin toward the island.

"It's a matter of national security."

Henry's curiosity was undeterred. "Then what happened to your hand?"

"Line of duty," Ben said.

Impressed, Henry turned the key, roaring the engine to life. Within minutes, Henry had quickly moved Ben closer to the castle so he could investigate a crime scene twenty-five years in the making.

CHAPTER 33

Warm water sprayed on them with each bounce of the fiberglass bow against the river. Henry docked at the island's river platform; Ben dismounted, managing to withhold the groan caused by the muscle strain in his lower back and legs.

"Thanks for the lift. I'll find my own way back," Ben said.

Henry nodded, letting go of the dock and floating back a few feet before accelerating toward Alex Bay's shoreline.

Perched on tall, wooden beams, Starr Island's security lights made Quill Castle look even taller than Ben had remembered. If the impressive exterior restoration of the grounds were any indication of the interior renovations, Ben thought, the castle must not look anything like the ramshackle structure it had decades ago.

He double-timed it through the iron gates while the Italian gardens of white phlox, scarlet gardenia and purple delphinium lining the stone walkway guided him to officials standing on the circular floor of a marble gazebo.

"You got here quickly, Agent Franklin. I'm Hollis Walker, Alex Bay Police Chief. He continued introductions for the group. "Roxie Sataro of *The River Gazette*, Taytum Dunn, Jefferson County Coroner." They exchanged nods and handshakes.

"It is not often I see the police and press visit a crime scene together," Ben said.

The Chief nodded. "We thought it wise to team up when releasing details to the public. We all know each other here. This case is personal."

Ben nodded. "Too much tragedy for these families, for this community."

Hollis clarified the significance of Ben's presence to the women. "He was the FBI's lead investigator of Brian and Patty's disappearance in 1990."

Ben grinned. "You have done your homework."

The coroner's phone dinged. Taytum read the text and excused herself.

"I need to start by claiming jurisdiction over this crime scene," Ben said. "Anything I say, anything you see, all of it, remains officially off the record. All details will be released via press release from our Syracuse office."

They nodded.

"My boss was the reporter who originally covered their disappearance," Roxie said. "Opal Schatz."

That's why her name sounded familiar, Ben thought.

"Listen. I need to tell you something else. The details of what I tell you will be emailed to you within the hour for release to the public."

He had their attention.

"Earlier today, Luke Annetti shot himself in the head with a blank bullet."

Hollis dropped his head and blessed himself.

Roxie set her hand on Hollis's shoulder, comforting him. "Is he dead?"

Ben shook his head. "He's still in ICU. I'll get hourly updates on his condition." He paused to let that sink in, then addressed Roxie. "Before he shot himself, he told me that letters about the case had been sent to the newspaper over the years. Is that true?"

"We keep a box in the safe and throw the letters in it when they arrive."

Ben took an aggressive step toward her. "Every possible and probable piece of evidence *should* have been reported to the FBI. Immediately."

Roxie squared her shoulders. "We call. No one comes."

Hollis stepped between them. "Let's take it easy. I understand that tensions are high. Luke always believed his son and Patty Flanagan were inside the castle. He never gave up on that. In fact, we found him out here on numerous occasions after Luke had triggered the castle's alarm system. We never officially arrested him because he never took or damaged anything. He just wanted to search for his son."

Ben looked up at the castle's turrets and saw what Luke Annetti had known. That the magnificent structure before him was more than a castle, it was a tomb.

"Take me to them," Ben said.

Once they were in the gift shop and about to approach the crime scene, Hollis explained the risks.

"The boards are brittle. More might break. We're figuring out how to stabilize the scene to extricate the bodies. We marked a safe spot to stand with silver tape."

Ben nodded. He took a few steps into the secret room, stopped on the X, and stared down at the skeletal remains of Brian Annetti and Patty Flanagan. His voice faded when he spoke. "They were here the whole God-damned time."

Hollis handed Ben binoculars, and Ben took them and focused the eyepiece onto broken bones and dented skulls.

"I see something near Brian's body," Ben said. "Some kind of papers, maybe?"

"We think those are blueprints tucked under his shirt, maybe the ones that had gone missing from the construction site back then."

Ben made a connection. "Luke Annetti worked on the construction crew back then. Maybe Brian found them and took Patty on a real-life treasure hunt." He took a step back.

"Speaking of that," Hollis said, "we found these hidden at the bottom of a porcelain vase on Ellie's nightstand." He held up an evidence bag containing a pearl necklace and ruby bracelet. "Mac says he has never seen them before."

"Terrific," Ben said dryly, returning his attention to the newly discovered teens. "There is no way to get someone down there now?"

"No, there is not," a deep voice said. Ben turned to see a man with an uncanny resemblance to the thick-bearded Grizzly Adams enter the room leading a small group of flannel-clad men.

"I'm the FBI," Ben said. "Who the hell are you?"

"Doug Manley of the Adirondack Mountain Terrain Rescue. This is my crew." As though they were a grown-up boy band gone naturally gnarly, each man put his hands on his hips with impressive synchronicity. "We're here to do a safety assessment. Boys came in from Gananoque, Brockville, Clayton and Lake Placid for this." He nodded to the gear stacked in a bucket – hollow scaffolding poles, locking carabiner clips, nylon ropes, and a basket stretcher.

This presentation made Ben smile. "On whose authority?"

"Mine," Hollis said. "Being located on the cusp of the Adirondack Mountains, we handle lots of mountain rescues under treacherous conditions from stone ledges to narrow caves. Inexperienced tourists get themselves trapped in difficult places, and even experienced climbers slip now and then. I didn't know you were on your way when I called them."

Ben could only nod in frustration.

Grizzly spoke up. "Singer Castle, down river, had multiple hidden entrances and exits used for cargo ship deliveries. We are looking to see if the same is true for this castle. It would be wiser to wait."

Ben didn't smile back. "Let me be clear. No one is going to look for anything anywhere. This crime scene has likely been contaminated for twenty-five years, and we're not going to add to that now. We don't know why the kids are down there or how they got there." He turned to Hollis. "I understand that this is an emotional case, that everyone wants answers to painful questions, but I need your patience. I want everyone out of this room and off these grounds. The FBI's Forensic Team will have their work cut out for them."

Grizzly smirked.

Ben took one last look at the intertwined skeletons and wrestled with the thought of Luke Annetti perhaps never knowing that his son had been found.

"Damn this all to hell," he said.

CHAPTER 34

Ben and Hollis stood side by side, watching the local and county investigators retreat to the waiting boats.

"Who was arrested?" Ben said.

"Ellie McAllister," Hollis said. "The wife of the groundskeeper."

"I remember her."

"Yeah. She said she locked them in."

Ben shook his head. "She said those actual words?"

Hollis nodded.

Ben spotted Roxie heading toward the dock. He called out to her. "Roxie! I'll stop by your office first thing in the morning to pick up that box."

Roxie had only time to nod before an officer shooed her down the path.

"The Sherriff will take us back whenever we want," Hollis said. "I'm not ready for the media circus tomorrow. Can you walk me through the day they disappeared?"

"I can do better than that. I'll show you."

Ben led Chief Walker over the lowered drawbridge and through the stone chapel to the river's edge. He pointed out the key changes in the landscape since the teens first disappeared. "That entire area was under construction back then. The dock was stacked with pallets of cobblestone for the walkways and ditches were being dug for the plumbing system by the clock tower. It was a mess."

"Where was the canoe?" Hollis asked.

Ben looked down at his feet. "Right here."

"The canoe could not have been washed up this far onto land. It had to have been pulled."

"The backpack contained only two items." Ben recited the items from memory. "Half a pack of cinnamon gum and a still-sealed condom." He looked at the castle. "Initially, we believed they were in there. We even brought in Pearl."

"Pearl?" Hollis asked.

"A yellow lab, the first police dog in the United States who had been exclusively trained for cadaver searches. In '74, she found the body of a Syracuse college student in a hidden grave four feet deep. I brought her and her handler to the castle, but Pearl found nothing, which made it even more frustrating."

"Why more?" Hollis said.

"The primary blueprints for the castle had gone missing. You know that Luke Annetti was the construction foreman back then," Ben said. "On the day of their disappearance, Luke frantically searched for the blueprints so investigators could cover every inch of the castle, but he never found them," Ben said. "Looks like they were with Brian the whole time."

A distant moan silenced their conversation. Both men moved their hands to their sidearms and turned toward the direction of the noise. Ben used his silver index finger to point east, leading them down the walkway to the island's electric powerhouse that had been built to resemble a mini castle, complete with four turrets sitting atop four stout, stone columns. They heard another moan as they rounded a Medieval-like clock tower that rose from the underwater shoal.

And then they saw them floating.

One alive. One dead.

A common black loon bleated an eerie, wavering wail in an attempt to rouse his dead mate from the dark, shallow water. His long, curved neck pushed his grim yodel up his throat, releasing it while poking his beak at her white feathers, hoping for a returning hoot but hearing none.

Hollis and Ben stared down at the loons.

"Just a dead bird," Hollis said.

Ben's voice fell to a whisper. "Bad luck."

"The case?" Hollis said.

"Finding a dead loon."

CHAPTER 35

Rosa wasn't manning the front desk at the Historical Society on Ash's next visit. The attendant on duty wore earphones and bobbed his head to a loud bass beat, waving his hand at Ash to head to the archives without a visitor tag.

Once back in the Quill room, he dropped his messenger bag on a table and went straight to the *Buildings & Grounds* section, pulling down binders stuffed with purchase orders issued for construction materials. After cross-referencing his list of twenty staff members with employee rosters of the construction team, he stared at his list of five names.

Evan Burnett
Edwin Francis
Edward Longfellow
Elijah Morris
Everett Mosley

From there, he bore through paystub files and accounting ledgers, double and triple checking names, trying to find which staff members, if any, worked at the Thousand Islands House *and* on the construction of Quill Castle. After hours of tedious attention, Ash had whittled his list down to just one name. He tried to think of what to do next, on how to proceed with his findings. But instead of crafting a new plan, Ash yawned. He tried but couldn't keep his chin from dropping to his chest. And for the next hour, slumped in a wooden chair, he dreamt of his new view of Griffin and Faith Quinn's opulent lifestyle at the height of the Gilded Age.

Cymbals crashed, tubas boomed, and drums rat-tat-tatted John Philip Sousa's "Stars and Stripes Forever" on the back lawn of the glitzy Thousand Islands House, a long, two-story hotel, to honor the arrival of Manhattan's wealthiest. The new rail line had transformed the cumbersome trip from the city to the sticks into a three-hour catered jaunt for those wanting to escape the weekend to riverside luxury.

A crowd of locals, cheering the arrival of each black-fringed horse-drawn carriage, served as giddy spectators. Tuxedo-dressed drivers jumped down to open carriage doors, offering a gloved hand as a firm guide to the hotel walkway. Men in waistcoats and women in minks, happy to breathe the crisp air of respite away from city life, waved to the crowd. Servants in black and white fitted uniforms were busy grabbing leashes of Airedales and handles of silk-lined hat boxes. With a gentle tilt of his head, the maître d' glided among the new arrivals offering glasses of bubbling champagne. When the doorman raised his hand, the crowd fell silent. In a booming voice, he made the announcement. "Now presenting Mr. and Mrs. Griffin Quill."

More cheers erupted. A tall, graying Griffin Quill stepped forward, smiling at the crowd. He slid his hand behind the back of his young wife, Faith, and together they climbed the hotel staircase. With each step, she lifted the hem of her shirt-waisted dress. They turned, waving to the crowd.

Boom! Faith's string of pearls and ruby bracelet glistened in the photographer's flash.

Griffin turned to his wife. "Happy fourteenth anniversary, darling," he said. Griffin took Faith's hand into both of his, raised it to his lips, and set a soft kiss on her skin. He looked into her eyes, drinking in her beauty. A yell from a photographer to look his way did not make him look away from his beloved.

Faith smiled. "I love the city, but I love it here more. This is where I belong."

The explosion of the camera flash broke the spell.

He pulled away. "To think we were lunching three hours ago at the Waldorf. Griffin looked at his gold pocket watch. "Carnegie should be here soon."

"The new high-speed rail is everything you said it would be," Faith said. "A Thousand Islands. A thousand dreams."

Ash's dream then shifted. His vibrant, jovial images of welcoming grand socialites to Alex Bay dissolved into a dimmer setting at the boathouse, where a lit cupola cast its faint light on the docks below.

Faith Griffin took cautious steps forward in the near darkness. She stepped back in fright at a lantern roaring to life; Everett's bronzed face glowed in the new light.

They found each other like magnets finding their mates. Their kiss electrified the pair, each clutching the other's neck and shoulders. Their hands grabbed; their throats moaned.

Everett whispered to his love. "I can't lose you again. Stay."

"I tried to tell him," Faith replied, shame lacing her words.

Everett pulled back. "So, nothing has changed."

"Everything has changed," she urged.

"Not if I must live my days without you."

Faith was insistent. "With the new rail, Manhattan is an afternoon trip. I can be here more often; I *will* be here more often."

Everett turned his back on her, growling in frustration. "The thought of that old man still having you." He turned to her, grabbing her by the shoulders. "Listen to me. It's not your fault. You were just a girl when your father sold you off to Griffin."

She broke from his grip, offended. "He did not sell me."

Everett wouldn't be swayed. "I've heard the stories from the crew, and this isn't a secret. Your husband was being wooed by your father to work for him. When Griffin hesitated, he sweetened the deal by adding you."

A whimper escaped Faith's lips.

Everett leaned in. "You were a fourteen-year-old girl. He's practically twice your age."

Faith shook her head, again, pushing him away. "Griffin adores me."

"You want to know what that bastard is doing for you now?" Everett stepped to the window and pointed toward the river. "It's too dark to see now, but in a few years, you'll see a castle straight out of a fairy tale rise into the sky from behind those trees in the center of Starr Island."

Faith smirked. "You're joking." Her eyebrows fell in concern when Everett didn't laugh.

"I only know about it because I'm the one who checks the manifest as materials arrive here for transport to the castle, something I surely could never give you," Everett said.

Faith took his hands into hers, but distant children's voices calling for their mama interrupted them.

"Here, my darlings!" Faith called back. "I am here." She ran out to find Griffin, Jr. and Cecelia, leaving Everett standing alone in the dark.

Ash jerked awake, then used his knuckles to rub his eyes in circles. He looked at his wrist.

Vivian will be worried, he thought.

With a swift swipe of his arm, he pushed files into a return bin and headed for the exit. He didn't need any written reminders of the one name he felt was now branded on his brain – Everett Mosley.

CHAPTER 36

A potent whiff of French toast, grilled potatoes and onions, cinnamon rolls and bacon roiled under the noses of hungry patrons. An hour after the FBI forensics team arrived and an hour before sunrise, Ben and Hollis sat in a booth at The Castle Café, the only Alex Bay restaurant open 24/7. They shoveled in mouthfuls of eggs and home fries, washed down by gulps of coffee.

Ben wiped the sides of his mouth with a napkin. "I will be here for the duration of the investigation. The office booked me at the Bijou House on Sisson Street."

"Good. You'll be just a block from the department," Hollis said.

Ben rubbed the bridge of his nose. "How do I explain this to the public? How could no one have found them?" Ben said. "Not members of the construction crew, not any of the constant visitors milling around."

Hollis knew the answer. "The renovation project was divided into eight regions. That shaft was in region eight, the last zone. Funding delays come and go, so progress starts and stops."

"It's been twenty-five years for Christ's sake."

"When we have a Democratic president, the funding floods in. With Republican presidents, that money dries up."

Ben knew this, how grants followed the party in charge. "So, politics directly impacted this investigation. Wonderful."

The police chief saw that the FBI agent needed some good news.

"Listen," Hollis said. "You can trust Opal at *The River Gazette*."

Ben smirked. "Trusting the press usually bites me in the ass. And that is the last thing I need right now."

Hollis defended his statement. "I'm just saying that Opal understands the sensitivity of this case." He leaned in. "Seriously. You *can* trust her."

Ben's phone chimed. He read the text to Hollis. "Luke Annetti is out of surgery. The doctors are optimistic."

Hollis blessed himself.

Ben blew out the tension that had been locked in his lungs. "I will keep you posted. But for now, I want to talk to your trustworthy editor about those letters."

CHAPTER 37

"So, I'm going to be a dad," Jasper Winsk said.

"More like I'm going to be a mom," Ruby clarified, seeing that her correction tightened his smile. "A twenty percent chance of the embryo taking was pretty low, so I guess I got lucky."

Long-time friend and colleague of Ruby, Jasper had opened his shop – Jazzy Tattoos – ten years ago. He was the only one she would trust to transform her back's birthmark into the work of art it was today. He was the only one she had confided in about her desire to become a mother. And then within three months, an agreement had been made, a contract signed, and a baby produced.

"Congratulations." He cleared his throat. "I have to head out now, so maybe we can catch up later."

Ruby took the hint. Despite Jasper's lackluster response, Ruby wanted to celebrate, choosing to make the hour-long trip back to Alex Bay tonight to tell the woman she loved about their new future.

After the seventh police cruiser sped by her on I-81N, Ruby used her Bluetooth to call her mom.

Opal picked up on the first ring. "Can't talk right now," she whispered.

"Mom. Do not hang up. What the hell happened? Are you okay?"

Opal's voice remained low. "I'm fine. Listen to me. Two bodies were found in Quill Castle. They were Brian and Patty."

Ruby let the words sink in. She knew she needed to let her mother do her job. "Love you."

"Love you, back," Opal said. The line went dead.

Seeing the stream of police cars and media vans clogging the Alex Bay exit, Ruby passed it by and took the next exit before doubling back to make it home to Hyo.

Using the key Hyo had given her, she arrived quietly, undressed, and slid into bed, wrapping her arms around her girlfriend's waist.

"Hmmmm." Hyo was only half awake.

"I have some news," Ruby breathed.

"Hmmmm."

Ruby listened to her hum turn into a snore. She slipped out of the bed, threw on Hyo's robe, and headed to the kitchen to make a pot of decaf coffee.

An hour later, Hyo walked out into the kitchen rubbing her forehead. "You are a sight for sore eyes. I thought you were staying in Syracuse last night."

Ruby handed Hyo a cup of coffee, then kissed her. "Plans changed." They sat at the table.

"I was really out," Hyo said. "Did you say you had news or was I dreaming?"

"I've been thinking about having kids," Ruby said honestly.

Hyo laughed. "Oh, you don't want any of those. All they do is not listen and hurt themselves and fill their parents with unrelenting bouts of hard-core fear."

Ruby frowned. "I thought you loved kids. I assumed you would want to have some of your own."

"I love *caring for other people's kids*," she said. "That's enough for me. I could never handle having to live with the daily worry that they could drown or get into an accident or cut off a finger. No way. That's not for me." Hyo sipped her coffee, grimacing at its flavor. "This is terrible. Tastes like decaf."

"Oh," was the best Ruby could muster.

"What?"

"I'm pregnant."

Hyo froze. "As in *pregnant* pregnant?"

Ruby nodded.

"Well, I know I'm not guilty of causing that," Hyo said.

Ruby spoke quickly, keeping her voice light. "You know, Jasper, in Syracuse? You met him before. He said he would be my sperm donor and signed a contract relinquishing his paternal rights. A doctor in Syracuse did the procedure two weeks ago, and I'm pregnant. Just like that. The doctor considers it a miracle."

Hyo stared at her.

Ruby continued. "I got the call yesterday after the meeting that the IVF worked." She opened and closed her hands to imitate fireworks. "I am forty-five years old, and I consider this a miracle, too."

Hyo listened, then stared at her feet. She blinked before looking up at Ruby. "This is not something we ever talked about. You found a sperm donor, signed a contract, and never thought to mention any of it to me?"

"What the hell? Am I the *only* one happy about this baby?" Ruby whined.

Hyo set down her coffee. "I am quite sure I can't be the 'us' you had expected in this scenario. I'm sorry. I've never even considered raising a child."

Without another word shared between them, Ruby stomped into the bedroom and dressed, then stomped out of the bedroom, slamming the front door behind her. She was damned if she was going to apologize, damned if she was going to explain herself. When Ruby reached the sidewalk, she thought just one sentiment:

Looks like I have a new Plus One.

CHAPTER 38

Ruby shouted "fuck" when she couldn't find her debit card in her purse to purchase lousy-tasting decaf coffee a donut joint drive-thru. She yelled it again when she dropped her keys on the sidewalk outside *Tats and Brews*. The third time, she screamed it at the top of her lungs after knocking over several bottles of ink that crashed to the floor behind her workstation.

Her soul sank when she heard the bells ring on the entrance door. The last thing she wanted at that moment was a customer. *"It's not even nine o'clock,"* she thought. She didn't even look up when offering up a lame "How can I help you?" toward the lobby.

"Hello, my dear," Enzo said.

She turned toward the door. "Mr. Kennedy," Ruby said. "What brings you by?"

"My dear. I've known you since you were a little girl. Call me Enzo," he said, all the while considering if one of her breasts would fit into the cup of his hand.

"Ok, Mr. Kennedy," she said, evaluating the mess of ink and glass at her feet. "Just give me a minute, and I'll be right with you." She grabbed a small plastic dustpan and brush and bent down to do a quick cleanup.

Enzo didn't want to wait, though, so he didn't stay in front of the counter. He needed answers. Listening to Bree's excitement at the morning newspaper was too much for him to bear. The kids being found and Ellie arrested. *What would Ellie say? Were his days numbered?* He slipped behind the counter and stood just inches from Ruby, inhaling her scent.

When Ruby's Spidey sense kicked in, she reacted instinctively, launching herself backward, ramming into Enzo and sending him stumbling back until ten feet separated them.

"Jesus, Mr. Kennedy. You scared me. Why don't you have a seat over there in the waiting area?"

"I'm sorry. It's my fault. I didn't want to lose my courage."

His comment caught Ruby's attention. "Courage for what?"

He held out his scarred right hand. "Is there anything you can do about this?"

Ruby took his hand into hers, sending jolts of electricity through his palm. She rubbed her thumb over the half-moon, jagged scar. "What bit you?"

"Nothing. It was a bad cut."

Lying about a scar wasn't rare, Ruby thought. She learned long ago not to push. "How long have you had it?"

"Twenty-five years to the day," he said. "I slipped on the dock the night those kids disappeared and had it stitched up in the emergency room. Can't believe they were found last night," he said.

"I heard," Ruby said. "I talked with Mom earlier."

Enzo nodded. "The whole town's abuzz. And I was shocked to learn that Ellie McAllister was arrested for murder. Did Opal say that Ellie actually killed Brian and Patty?" Enzo asked, fishing for details.

"I only spoke to her for a minute, and I only know what you know." Ruby kept examining his scar. "It's an awkward shape but quite smooth. You will have lots of options."

He laughed a little. "I have to say that I haven't been able to stop thinking about you since the board meeting," Enzo said. "I thought I could benefit from your expertise."

"Absolutely," she said, stoked that she would have another set of 'before and after' photos to post in her portfolio. She rummaged around for a binder. "Here. Look through this. Let me know if you see anything you like."

Enzo didn't open the book. "I already know what I want," he said. "A rosary."

Ruby flipped open her sketchbook to the religion section and watched Enzo's eyes light up when he saw his options. "This one would stand out best in red, but the beads can be any color," Ruby said.

"Black. I want black beads."

"Do you want to think it over for a few days?"

He shook his head. "No. I'm certain."

Ruby nodded and led him to her station. They sat across from each other, a metal light shining brightly down on his hand. She held her phone over his hand, about to snap a photo, but he drew it back.

"Why do you need a photo?" he asked.

"Common procedure," she said. "Clients often like to compare the before and after."

"I trust you," Enzo said. "There's no need to remind me of what I'm trying to forget."

Ruby nodded, setting down her phone and slipping on thin nylon gloves. Positioning his wrist at an angle, she wiped the fleshy part of his hand with antiseptic.

"All right, Mr. Kennedy. I'm going to start now. Let me know if you want me to stop. Just try not to flinch."

"Don't worry," he said. "I don't flinch."

CHAPTER 39

Opal had managed to get the new front page to the printer *and* four hours of sleep before returning to *The River Gazette* at nine.

She watched a determined man pass by her front window and push open the lobby door. *This had to be him,* she thought. She crossed her arms and squared her shoulders.

Speaking before Ben could even introduce himself, Opal took control of the conversation, speaking before Ben could introduce himself. "So, you are Mr. FBI guy who thought telling Luke Annetti you were closing his son's case was a good idea."

Ben instantly remembered her as the diligent, feisty reporter from the initial investigation decades ago. She had remained a woman with fire in her belly though her maroon birthmark no longer matched her once auburn hair. Ben took ownership of his actions. "I am."

And with that admission, Opal slapped him across the face. Hard.

Ben blinked and offered no defense. In some way, he felt he deserved it, that her outrage was justified.

"Luke Annetti is a good man. The timing was unfortunate," he said, suddenly noticing her shoulder muscles twitch and her torso sway slightly, two of the tell-tale signs of a fainting woman. He stepped forward and tried to steady her by sliding his mechanical hand behind her back. Ben did not realize how wrong he had read the scene until a second slap struck his face. "What the hell?" he said.

Lines of reddening fury ran down Opal's neck. For every step she took closer to him, he took one back.

"First, they were runaways. Then, they accidentally drowned. Did you know Suzie Annetti died last year?" Opal's words pelted him like bullets. "Patty's parents fled the country to try to escape the pain. And don't give me some lame-ass sob story that you were doing all you could because, Agent Franklin, you could have done more. Luke Annetti could have been your best resource." She jammed her index finger into his chest during her next five words. "Have you thought of that?"

Now backed against the wall, Ben had a new vantage point to observe Opal's face – her glimmering hazel eyes, the soft curve of her lips – traits he hadn't admired on any woman since Gwen. He was so entranced by this silver-stranded spitfire that he missed those tell-tale signs of a fainting woman.

Opal's knees gave out, and she hit the ground with a thud.

Ben thought just one thing: *Shit.*

Half an hour later, Opal and Ben sat across from each other at the conference table. Ben drank hot coffee from a pirate mug, and Opal sipped water from a plastic bottle.

"You really should get checked out at the hospital," Ben said.

Opal shook her head. "It happens whenever I feel claustrophobic. The events of the past twelve hours, finding Brian and Patty and Ellie being arrested, made it feel like walls were closing in on me."

"I can relate to that," Ben said.

Opal took another sip of water. "I do remember you," she said. "We were both starting our careers when we first met at the crime scene."

Ben nodded. "You have aged better than I have."

Opal tried to hold back the blush.

"Tell me about the letters," he said.

"I have a whole box of them, sent to me from psychics and private investigators, all promising they could find Patty and Brian alive. I stopped calling your regional office a decade ago because there was never any follow-through." She stopped herself from beginning a second tirade of blame. "I can get it from the safe." Opal wobbled when she stood.

"Whoa," Ben said, jumping to his feet. "How about I get the box, and you stay right there? I don't need you going into a small, confined space right now."

Opal nodded and pointed down the hall. "I took out the subscription checks to deposit at the bank earlier, so it should still be open. The letters are on the right in a brown box."

Ben pulled out thin, blue gloves from his pocket and entered the safe. He returned with a cardboard box full of envelopes. "I can't explain why an agent never collected these. It goes against protocol. I've arranged for a courier to pick these up and transport them directly to our forensics crime lab in Syracuse," he said, sitting across from her. "You will no longer be ignored. I promise you."

Opal nodded. The two fell into an awkward silence until Opal broke it.

"Did Ellie tell you anything?"

Ben gave her a sympathetic look. "Off the record?"

Opal grinned. "Of course. Off the record."

Ben sat back. "She won't talk to me, and we will likely have to transfer her to a psychiatric center for evaluation."

"Let me try." Opal leaned forward. "With you there, of course. Ellie said she wanted to tell me what happened. It's in my statement."

Ben nodded and evaluated her request. "I'll consider it. I'll be in touch as soon as I know our next step. I'm staying at the Bijou House."

"It's nice there. You'll like it."

"I hope so; it's on the company's dime," he said, immediately feeling foolish. He pushed open the door and walked halfway out.

"Ben," Opal called. He stopped and turned to her. "Sorry I slapped you."

It was Ben's turn to blush. "Sorry I made you faint."

CHAPTER 40

Dr. Jin Byong knew his fitful night of sleep had been triggered by his interaction with Enzo Kennedy. He had spent those precious predawn hours wrestling with his intense dislike for a man with whom he had little regular interaction or contact. It wasn't just the ER visit years ago that was stuck in his craw. It was something else. But what?

He rolled over in bed to look at his clock, then calculated the time difference with London; he tried to catch Maya before her research group met to discuss the day's plan over butteries and kippers. He dialed his wife's number using the proper international coding.

When she picked up, Jin wasted no time. "Tell me why we don't like Enzo Kennedy."

Maya deflected his request. "You don't miss me? You don't want to know how my Alzheimer's research is going? What gives?"

He knew she was right. "I'm sorry. I didn't sleep well. I ran into Kennedy yesterday and can't put my finger on my intense dislike for that guy. Why don't I remember?"

"Maybe you should be part of my study."

"Ha, ha. I'm not wrong about this. Am I?"

Maya hesitated before answering. "Hyo is the reason we don't like him."

"Hyo?" he said.

She gave him a clue. "Junior year."

Jin closed his eyes to think back twenty-five years.

"The art lessons, dear."

Jin's eyes opened. "The art lessons. I remember now. Bree Kennedy was her favorite teacher."

Maya's voice softened. "Hyo was so excited to begin private evening art lessons from Bree at her home."

Jin proved his memory was intact. "After the first lesson, she came home in a fury. She threw her art supplies on the floor and stormed to her room. We didn't know what to do, what had happened."

Across the pond, Maya was nodding. "She showered for over an hour."

"We asked her to tell us what was wrong, to trust us," he said.

"We did," Maya said. "All Hyo would say is that she would never step foot in the Kennedy house again, that Bree was a fraud and Enzo was a pig."

"We asked if she was hurt, if we should call the police," Jin said. "Do you remember what she did?"

"Of course, I do," Maya said. "She laughed. And then she said, 'I'm not the one who's damaged.'" Maya paused. "A few days after that, she started getting college acceptance letters and never brought it up again."

"And it was a year after that Enzo came into the ER the night Brian and Patty disappeared; I wasn't pleased I was the one who had to treat him."

"Why are you curious about Enzo Kennedy now? Has something happened in Alex Bay?"

Jin rolled back, resting his head on the pillow. "Tell your colleagues to put your kippers on hold. This will take a while, love."

By late morning, after Jin had updated his wife about the discovery of the teens' bodies, he repeatedly yawned on his drive to the Medical Records Department of Alex Bay Hospital. He was confident that a few cups of Harriet's coffee would pep him up for the rest of the morning, but when he rounded the lobby corner and saw his office dark, he realized this was the week his secretary would be in Pittsburgh visiting her grandkids. Jin would have to sit front and center this week, answering phones and managing requests. He yawned again.

Jin fumbled for his keys and flicked on the lights, dropping his leather bag on Harriet's vacant desk. He went right to the filing cabinets and returned with an olive-colored folder, plopping it on her desk and sitting in her chair. Its label was clear – *Enzo Kennedy*.

He opened the file and picked up the photo he had taken of Enzo's injury twenty-five years ago and remembered telling the Kennedys that night that the injury did not look like one caused by a fall.

Only after Bree left the examination room insulted over his needling questions did Jin ask Enzo for the truth: "Who bit you?"

"I fell on the dock," Enzo had said. "I should have been more careful in the rain."

The two men had stared at each other until Bree returned. "I gave my insurance card to the girl up front. How many stitches do you think he'll need?" She had crossed her arms over her chest.

"Between fourteen and twenty," Jin had said. "It's a deep cut. I called in Dr. Halifax to sew you up. He's the plastic surgeon on call tonight."

An orderly pulled aside the hanging drape and pushed in a wheelchair. "They're ready for you upstairs, Mr. Kennedy."

Bree had kissed his cheek, and Enzo had eased himself into the wheelchair and was whisked down the hall into a waiting elevator.

Jin had turned to Bree. "Hyo is a senior this year, and you were her favorite teacher for most of high school."

Bree had pursed her lips. "I had high hopes for her as an artist, but I guess she turned her interests elsewhere this year. Such a shame."

When another long yawn overcame Jin, he dropped the photo onto the open file and headed down the hall to the hospital cafeteria for a cup of coffee, not bothering to lock up.

Claudine could not believe her luck. She had been watching Jin from behind a magazine in the waiting room directly across from Medical Records. Because Claudine had worked regularly with the hospital, transporting patients to and from Manor Oak, she knew the office's inner workings and of Harriet's trip to Pittsburgh. In fact, it had been something Harriet had said to her that made Claudine hatch a plan to remove Daniel's toxicology report from his medical file. Harriet had said, "Lawyers request what seem like random test results, but then they use the results to establish patterns in court."

Patterns.

Claudine believed that she had already dodged a bullet a year ago when Opal took her advice to *Let Daniel Rest in Peace*, convincing her to not consent to an autopsy. Without one, the coroner ordered and ran a standard tox report, one that did not specifically test arsenic levels. But Claudine wondered if a *pattern* could be drawn later in a courtroom. If there was no solid connection between Claudine with Daniel back then, there's no reason to suspect Claudine now. She thought of the steps she had already taken to protect herself – reporting Opal to corporate by claiming she was still grieving over her husband's death, filing a harassment report with the police, alerting the community of her potential danger and instability. People would see Claudine as the victim, proving a sympathetic witness if ever called to the stand. And when she returned to her home scot-free, she would focus her attention on finding ways to punish Howard.

But Claudine was no fool. She knew she needed to be careful, especially with that hotshot FBI agent in town. Word was that he solved impossible crimes.

Only after Jin yawned his way down the corridor and turned the corner did Claudine slip into the office. She headed straight back to the file cabinets lining the back wall and pulled open the 'S' drawer.

Between quick breaths, she located Daniel Schatz's file, found the toxicity report, and stuffed the report into her pocket. After tucking the file back into the drawer, she was almost home free when she spotted the photo on Jin's desk.

The image looked familiar, she thought. The name typed on the page beneath the photo jogged her memory. Everyone in town knew how responsible Enzo had felt for not visiting Ellie McAllister the night the teens had disappeared, the night his friend, Mac, was out of town. Enzo had told the same story, over and over again – if he had not slipped on the dock, he might have seen something, heard something that could have helped the teens. Claudine remembered hearing how his guilt was consuming him. *Thank God he has Bree to get him through,* they had all said.

Claudine chided herself for pausing too long but suddenly found her legs frozen in place when she read three words scrawled across the bottom of the old photograph, the first word in capital letters: *HUMAN bite mark.*

Looking from side to side, finding the coast clear, she took her phone from her pocket and snapped a photo.

Patterns, she thought.

CHAPTER 41

An overripe tang of body odor snaked itself between iron bars and sanitized floors.

A uniformed police officer unlocked and slid open Ellie's cell door. Opal and Ben stepped inside before the iron door crashed shut behind them. The small square room held only a cot and a confessed killer. Ellie stood in the center of the holding cell, shifting her weight back and forth, chanting a repetitive phrase in random-pitched, frantic tones – "I can't ever tell. I can't ever tell. I can't ever tell." Her orange jumpsuit overpowered her pale skin, and her long gray hair, once braided, was unkempt and knotted.

Ellie's appearance matched the electronic mugshot Opal had received hours earlier. Readers, after seeing her friend's red-rimmed eyes, wild hair, and ghostly skin, would certainly draw the same grim conclusion that she, herself, had drawn: *Ellie McAllister is a madwoman.* As though running Ellie's mugshot in *The River Gazette* wasn't enough, Opal had read through the headlines of other newspapers carrying the story, from *The New York Times* to *The Los*

Angeles Times to *The Toronto Star*. Each one read like a death sentence.

Cold Case Cracked: Elderly Woman in Custody

Unlikely Suspect Confesses to 1990 Killing in Castle

A Killer Living Among Us

Opal stepped forward, taking her friend's hands into hers. "You're freezing." She turned to Ben. "Can she have a blanket and warm broth, please?"

He obliged and nodded to the guard who turned and disappeared down the hall.

"Ellie. It's Opal." She kept her voice low, trying to trigger a glimmer of recognition.

Ellie's eyes remained fluid, darting in different directions as she bleated, "I can't ever tell," seemingly unaware of her friend's efforts to help her.

Ben explained the legality of the moment. "She has to give consent to this interview or nothing she says will be admissible."

Opal eased her toward the cot, and to her relief, Ellie agreeably sat beside her. "Ellie, you showed me the secret room in the castle."

"I can't ever tell. I can't ever tell," Ellie said.

"You wanted to tell me. Last night, Ellie. You said you needed to tell me."

The guard returned with a blanket and cup of broth. Ben handed the cup to Opal, then went to Ellie and wrapped the blanket around her shoulders before stepping back to the barred entrance. Opal secured the broth in Ellie's hands. "Drink this. It will warm you up. You'll feel better."

Ellie obeyed her friend, gulping down the warm liquid. When done, she lowered her hands and looked at Opal. "We were friends once," she said softly.

"And we still are," Opal said, turning back to Ben for encouragement.

"Guard," Ben called out.

"No," Opal said. "Let's talk to her here."

"No way. This questioning needs to be recorded. I'm not going to jeopardize a decades-old case for comfort."

Opal sat back on her laurels. She knew he was right.

Ben gave the directive to the officer: "Take them to Interrogation Room #1."

Ellie had agreed to sign Ben's release, allowing the interview to continue without her lawyer present and for it to be recorded on the other side of a two-way mirror that took up most of an entire wall in the interrogation room. No more modern than the holding cell, this room contained a metal table surrounded by three chairs. Opal and Ellie sat across from Ben.

"Ellie," Opal began. "Ben is my friend, and he wants to help you. He's going to ask you some questions about last night. You sure that's okay?"

Ellie nodded.

Ben looked down at the questions he had compiled with Hollis's help and was surprised to see someone that had drawn a large X over all of them. At the bottom someone had written one simple statement: *Start at the beginning, Ellie.* He looked to Opal, who smirked and did a bad job feigning her innocence. In that moment, he chose to trust her tactic since she had made more progress than any agent had.

Ben spoke softly. "Start at the beginning, Ellie."

Ellie closed her eyes and rocked herself back and forth. She squeezed Opal's hand.

"It's okay, Ellie," Opal said.

And slowly, she began to tell her story.

"We had been married for four years, Mac and me, when we moved into Quill Castle so he could oversee the reconstruction and care for the building and grounds. He worked day and night while I tended the house, cooked meals, and pretended I was a princess living in a fairytale. We were so in love and talked of having enough children to fill all the castle's rooms."

She licked her lips.

"And then came the night I stayed at the castle alone. Mac had to go to Buffalo for a builder's conference. I told him I'd be fine for a night, but he wanted to protect me. I had practiced weaving a white ribbon into my hair braid to surprise Mac when he came back home the next day." Ellie's voice was hollow and distant, her memories more random. "I had also been expecting Enzo for dinner. Mac had asked him to check on me."

Opal turned to Ben, providing details of the backstory. "Enzo never made it out to check on her and has felt guilty about that his entire life."

Ellie blinked, her eyes settling on Ben.

Ben shifted in his seat.

"I was washing a plate in the sink when I thought I had heard a noise, like voices. I dropped the plate. It crashed to the floor."

"What startled you, Ellie?" Ben asked.

"I heard them. I saw them down there."

"How did they get there?" he said.

And without warning, Ellie threw back her head and screamed.

Opal tried to wrap her arms around her, to hold her, but Ellie's flailing arms pushed Opal to the ground. Ben hit the emergency button under the desk, sending guards rushing in. They restrained Ellie as she struggled for freedom.

With one quick motion, Ben lifted Opal off the floor and out the door. "Call a medic for the perp," he called to an officer, setting Opal down. "She needs to be checked out, too."

"No, I'm fine," Opal said. "When can I talk with her again?"

Ben needed a way to diffuse her eagerness. "The medical team needs time with her. I'm taking you to lunch."

"Just a few minutes more," she pleaded.

"Listen. While we were in there, the forensics team texted me. The lab found something in the letters that were sent to your newspaper. I'll get a call within the hour with the details."

Opal swayed slightly. "I need some air."

Ben pressed his good hand softly on the small of her back, then used his titanium hand to grasp her elbow, easing her toward the door.

"What are you doing?" Opal said.

"No way I'm losing you twice."

CHAPTER 42

Clanks of ceramic plates and jangles of clean silverware dominated the afternoon atmosphere when Ben and Opal entered The Castle Café at the end of the lunch rush. They slid into a booth in the back corner.

Chief Hollis spotted them while paying his check at the front register. He waved and stopped at their table to deliver some news. "The team got the kids out last night. The preliminary autopsy reports for Brian and Patty will be out tomorrow morning, but it looks like they both have broken necks. Their deaths were immediate."

To Opal he said, "That's off the record." To Ben he said, "I'll call you as soon as I have the official report."

"I appreciate that, sir," Ben said, shaking his hand.

"Yeah, thanks a lot," said Opal, smirking at Hollis.

A new text on Hollis's phone sent him hustling out the door.

Ben set his phone on the table so he could take Agent Ameth Baxter's call the moment it came in; she was the first boss he had

had who was quite a few years his junior. She kept her black hair pulled back so tightly that her eyes looked pinned open, able to blink only when necessary. She had earned Ben's respect when he had seen her take down a six-two, drunk biker, with a Kung Fu kick that had left the man pleading for his mommy. The only personal thing he knew about her – other than the fact she could kick his ass – was that she had a deep-seated love for pistachios. The sharp crack from the opening of the shelled nut radiated into his ear during their phone conversations.

But, right now, he needed to wait. He stared across the table at Opal, realizing that he was going to have to do something he hadn't done since Gail had died – have a meal with a beautiful woman.

They each ordered an omelet, home fries, and coffee. When the waitress asked if they wanted toast, they both replied "no" in unison.

"The potatoes cover my carb limit for the day," Ben said.

"Carbs work themselves into everything, don't they," Opal said, realizing she was terrible at making small talk. She listened to their spoons clink against the insides of the ceramic coffee mugs.

"So, you saved Buffalo," Opal began. "That's sure something."

He smiled. "I got lucky."

"How did you like being the center of attention, being on magazine covers and newspaper front pages everywhere?"

Ben growled. "Made me openly consider retirement," he said, sipping his coffee. "You'll find out for yourself soon enough. I heard about your AARP article."

"How?"

He laughed. "I've already learned that the rumor mill in Alex Bay is quite efficient."

"I bet you have," she chuckled. "I'm figuring it will be grand seeing my photo tucked between advertisements for hip replacements and hearing aids." She held up her coffee mug for a celebratory toast. Ben tapped his with hers, and for the next fifteen minutes, they talked like long-lost friends, their voices rich and real. To a stranger, they looked like an old married couple still in love.

They were so focused on each other that neither noticed the waitress refilling their coffee mugs. And neither of them noticed Claudine Schatz staring at them through the front window, her mouth agape.

"I read about your bionic hand," Opal said, "that you lost it early on in your career."

Ben nodded. "I was in my seventh year. It was a hostage situation gone very, very wrong. The scene was secured, but we didn't know the perp had a partner. His bullet embedded itself into my wrist, shattering every bone but stopping the bullet from penetrating the face of the nine-year-old girl I was carrying to safety. So that's a win in my book," he said.

She nodded, watching him take the last bite of his omelet and set down his fork.

In unison, they asked each other the same question: "Are you married?"

After their laughter faded, each provided the basic details.

"Daniel's death was sudden. My sister-in-law, Claudine, found him collapsed at our kitchen table during breakfast."

"I'm sorry," Ben said, his eyes softening in sympathy. "Gail had pancreatic cancer; I watched her die for six months."

Opal shook her head. "I'm sorry, too."

And then they didn't know what to say. It was as though Daniel and Gail were now ghostly embodiments at the table.

Opal cleared her throat. "Seeing their bodies, their remains, was difficult last night."

Ben missed Opal's tone shift from sympathetic to serious. "Oh, come on. Last night must have been a journalist's dream."

Opal shook her head. "No, no. It brought back the memory of the night we lost Ruby." She instinctively put her hand over her heart.

Ben kept his gaze on her, indicating he wanted to know the story.

"She must have been eight or nine," Opal said. "She had told us she was heading down to the river to skip some rocks at the docks. A little before dusk, we went looking for her, calling out her name, but she wasn't there. We tried to pretend that we weren't panicked for the sake of each other, but we were petrified. Daniel called down to the precinct and within minutes, police officers were canvasing the area. It was when I watched a police boat searching the river with a spotlight that I imagined my little girl dead, her body being pulled to the surface by a diver. That's when I first passed out, when I felt like my world was closing in on me."

Instinctively, Ben reached out and touched her hand.

"When I came to, it was Ruby's sweet face I saw first. Turns out, she had crawled into one of those wicker storage areas on our boat and fallen asleep on top of the life jackets. The sirens had woken her."

"That's a horror story with a happy ending if I've ever heard one," Ben said.

Opal pointed to her hair. "Daniel said I went gray overnight."

When Ben's phone rang, they snapped back into professionals, the federal investigator and the newspaper editor.

The phone was at Ben's ear in an instant. "What do you have for me?" He listened intently, never breaking eye contact with Opal. "Send me those." He ended the call.

"What?" Opal said.

Ben shook his head. "This must be off the record, Opal. The public cannot know yet."

Opal nodded. "Of course. I give you my word."

He returned a nod to confirm their understanding.

"Most of the mail in the box arrived near the anniversary of their disappearance, which is typical in highly publicized missing person cases. But there were similarities between some of the letters, so they tested the DNA from the envelope and found a match. Someone has sent you a letter every few years offering encouragement in finding Brian Annetti and Patty Flanagan."

"Who?" Opal said.

"That's where it gets interesting. In addition to Jefferson, the letters were mailed from three other nearby counties – Lewis, Oswego, and Oneida – with return addresses for streets that do not exist; each letter has a different handwriting style and contains no fingerprints, yet each has the same DNA under the flap. It doesn't match anyone in the system."

"But it's a lead," she said.

"It is a lead, and I have to go."

Ben scooted out of the booth, dropped cash on the table, and left. Now alone, Opal took out her notebook and jotted down every word Ben had said. She slid her reporter's notebook into her purse for safekeeping.

Out on the sidewalk, Ben dialed his boss who picked up on the first ring. "Talk to me, Baxter."

Ben heard the crack of a nut from the receiver. "The profiler says male, married, middle to upper class, employed in a white-collar job."

"And?" Ben said.

"He's a local."

CHAPTER 43

Howard thought it wise to spend the night at his office. It wasn't the first time he had chosen to pull some vinyl chairs from the lobby into his office, but he never felt more like a failure than he did right then. Failure as a husband. Failure as a brother. Failure as a father.

He sat at his desk tapping a pen on a sheet of pink copy paper normally used to print invoices. He had written several beginnings of sentences over the course of the early morning hours, but, after rereading them, thought they sounded like lame excuses piled atop each other in rambling confessions of shame. Each one, he crossed out with a thin line from his pen.

What words could adequately explain his lie?

When Ruby walked in carrying a cloth bag, Howard turned over the pink letter, keeping it face down.

"I got your text and came right….," Ruby said, stopping when she eyed his chin stubble and messy hair." What happened to you?"

"I pulled an all-nighter catching up on paperwork."

"Well, you look like shit, Uncle Howard," she said, handing the bag to him before plopping herself in a chair across from his desk. "Aunt Claudine stopped by to see me at the shop yesterday."

Howard felt hot vomit lurching up his esophagus. "She did?"

She knows, Howard thought. *She already knows.*

"And she brought me these," Ruby said, pointing at the bag.

Howard reached in and set the peach delicacies near the edge of his desk.

"She made them for Mom who happens to be quite busy right now," Ruby said. "I wouldn't want these to go to waste."

Howard pried for details. "So, Claudine didn't say anything else?"

Ruby snapped her fingers. "I almost forgot. She apologized for being such an asshole."

Howard started coughing. "I never expected that," he said between wheezes.

"That makes two of us," Ruby said. "So, what gives? Your text said you had to tell me something. I thought we could chat while stuffing our faces with peach pie." From her pocket, she whipped out two plastic forks.

Howard ran his finger over his lower lip but couldn't muster the courage to tell her the truth, that he was her biological father, that he was a coward, that he was nothing more than a fraud. His eyes darted to the pink letter. "Let's have some of that pie first. I can smell it from here."

Ruby didn't need any coaxing. Unsure if pregnancy hormones had already kicked in or if she simply couldn't resist her aunt's pie,

Ruby scooped up a forkful of crust and peaches and stuffed it into her mouth. After she swallowed, she pushed the tin toward Howard. "That is fucking delicious. Have some."

Howard followed suit, and, together, they passed the poisoned pie back and forth until only crust crumbs and a few splotches of peach goo remained on the bottom.

Ruby smacked her lips while gathering up the pie plate and forks and dropping them into the trash can. "That woman can cook." She looked at her uncle and frowned. "You okay? You look a little pale."

CHAPTER 44

Dr. Hyo Byong hated slow nights in the ER. She preferred an appendicitis attack with a side of stroke victims in place of watching the minutes tick by on the ward's circular clock, giving her ample time to play and replay, over and over, her conversation with Ruby. *Within an hour*, she thought, *they went from snuggling together in bed to breaking up. WTF?*

Hyo couldn't help but wonder. Did she, herself, share any blame for their relationship exploding into teeny tiny fragments of emotional debris? She wasn't the one who arranged for sperm to be inserted into her body without telling her girlfriend. She wasn't the one who told the love of her life, that, in addition to bringing home milk and bread from the store, that she was also bringing home a baby.

Time crawled.

Hyo was examining Connor Szymczak's X-rays and considering how to tell him that his baseball-playing days were over for the summer when she heard the ambulance's reverse warning beeps echo from the loading dock.

"I need help, stat!"

Hyo knew Sebastian Ramos's voice well. He was the night EMT who enjoyed giving and receiving playful banter. His voice tonight, though, indicated no joke.

"Male in his sixties. Found unconscious. Started vomiting en route. Began an IV at the scene." He looked at Hyo. "Doc, it's Howard Schatz." His voice stayed urgent. "Take him. I need to help Milo with the second vic." Sebastian disappeared through the swinging doors.

Hyo pushed the gurney into a curtained medical stall chock full of life-saving equipment. The head nurse secured the IV bag, plugged in cords from his blood pressure cuff, checked his oxygen levels, while Hyo listened to his heart through her stethoscope.

The two worked side by side in silence. Their swift, purposeful movements brought numbers and graphs to life in neon colors on the monitors perched around the victim.

"Look at his hands," the nurse said.

Howard's hands had sporadic brown, circular lesions that resembled small planters' warts.

Hyo leaned in close to Howard's face. "Howard, it's Dr. Byong. Can you understand me?" No response. She checked his pupils with a pen flashlight.

Howard moaned, his skin looking pasty and blanched. His eyelids struggled to lift themselves as he tried to force his desperate words out of his throat. "Help her first. Save Ruby."

Hyo blinked.

Sebastian pulled aside the drapery. "Vic 2. Female in her forties. Found unconscious. Vomited profusely at the scene. I have samples," he said, holding up a clear baggie of brown mush.

Hyo went to her side, not able to fully register Ruby's gray-tinted face; an oxygen mask covered her mouth and nose.

"What the hell happened?" Hyo called out.

"Doc. Looks like an overdose," he said. "We gave Narcan to both vics with no result. They both threw up their stomach contents."

Hyo's heart sank, the word overdose still hanging in the air. "Call in Dr. Allen. Get the lab down here. I want tox reports back asap."

The nurse nodded, dialing the lab.

"You better call in Lucas, too," Hyo said.

"From obstetrics? For what?"

"Vic two is pregnant."

CHAPTER 45

Bree's scream brought Enzo running into their kitchen. "What's wrong?" he said, keeping his gauze-wrapped hand behind his back.

His wife was on the phone listening intently to someone giving her shocking news. Bree sighed heavily, moaning at one point before nodding in agreement. "Of course. Yes. Yes. My God. Ok. Ok. Yes. I'm on my way." She ended the call.

"Who was that?" Enzo said.

"Opal. She said that Ruby and Howard were found unconscious. They're in the ER, and it's serious. The doctors are saying it might be some type of overdose."

"Overdose," Enzo said. "Should we head over to be with her?"

"No. Opal said there was nothing we could do at the hospital right now, but she asked me to do something else. She said she was about to head down to the police station to help that pushy FBI agent interview Ellie when she got the call about Ruby and Howard. She said Ellie had responded better with a friend in the room and asked if

I would take her place, that I should explain this to the agent when we get there."

Enzo felt his crotch warm at the thought of being in a room with Ellie. "Are you okay with being in a room with a murderer?" he asked.

"She's my friend, Enzo. "I want to help her."

Enzo grabbed his jacket. "I'll go with you."

"Good idea. Maybe seeing both of us, seeing our love for her, would help her relax."

"I bet you're right." Enzo slid on his jacket, quickly inserting his wrapped hand into its pocket.

Agent Franklin reviewed Mac's original statement with him in Interrogation Room #2.

"To summarize," Ben said, "you left for the conference in Buffalo at four on the morning of June 20 and returned at around eleven in the evening on June 21, which would have been Brian Annetti and Patty Flanagan's graduation day. You don't think anyone else visited Starr Island while you were gone."

"No. No one," he said. Mac scratched his temple. "I had asked Enzo to check on her, but…"

Ben looked through the statement. "I don't see that in your original statement."

"No, you wouldn't," Mac said. "Enzo told me he wasn't able to make it out there, that he had cut himself and ended up in the ER that night. To this day, he still thinks he might have seen something, heard something, that could have helped find Brian and Patty."

So I keep hearing, he thought.

A new voice entered the conversation from the doorway. "He sure does," Bree said, looking sympathetically at her husband standing beside her.

Enzo nodded his head slowly. Mac went to him and shook his hand.

"I'm FBI Agent Ben Franklin."

"Electrifying," Bree joked.

Ben let the joke pass before acknowledging them. "You are Enzo and Bree Kennedy?" he asked.

Mac nodded. "Bree and I have known Mac and Ellie our whole lives."

Enzo kept his wrapped hand in his jacket pocket.

"Opal called me and said to tell you that she couldn't make it," Bree said. "We are also friends with Ellie, so she thought just having us in the same room might keep her relaxed enough to answer your questions."

Ben's first thought was that he had put on cologne that morning, something he hadn't done for a decade, for nothing. Opal had found something else to do. She wasn't coming.

Bree was about to explain how Opal had to rush to the hospital for Ruby and Howard, but Agent Franklin's phone rang. He cut her off. "I'm sorry, but I have to take this." He excused himself to a corner, mumbled a few words, and returned to the couple.

"I tend to agree with you on this. Ellie did open up a little with Opal in the room, especially after hearing about some high school memories. I don't want to get your hopes up. If this doesn't work, we'll transport her to a psychiatric facility outside of Syracuse tonight."

Mac patted Enzo on the back. "You and I can wait in the lobby," he said.

"No," Enzo blurted. "I'm sorry, Mac. I'm not comfortable with Bree being in there without me. Is it okay with you if I go in with her?"

Mac looked at Ben for approval.

Ben nodded. "She won't say anything to me. Since she knows both of you very well, maybe your presence will help."

"I'll do whatever I can," Enzo said.

CHAPTER 46

Ellie sat in a metal chair and rested her folded hands on the long, gray table. She kept her eyes down. Bree sat beside her, Ben across from her, and Enzo sat propped in the chair at the end of the table.

Ben kept his voice low. "Mrs. McAllister, I'm Agent Franklin. I work with the FBI. Can you hear me?"

They waited for any type of acknowledgment but received none. Ben nodded to Bree to begin.

"It's Bree, love. One of the Quirky Quadruplets from way back when."

Ellie didn't move.

Bree continued. "We had second-period English together senior year and fifth-period lunch. Do you remember that? For lunch, we sat at a table with Enzo. He's right here, dear."

Ellie blinked. They all saw it. Bree looked at Ben, who nodded for her to continue.

"You were the maid of honor at our wedding," Bree said.

Almost imperceptibly, Ellie began rocking back and forth.

Bree nudged Enzo to join in by adding details from Memory Lane.

"I'm here, too, Ellie. You're safe here," Enzo said. "We want to help."

Ellie slowly raised her arms straight over her head and slammed them onto the metal table, causing them to jump. Her red-rimmed stare returned to the table. "It's all your fault," she whimpered to herself. "I did what I had to do. He hurt me," she said.

Ben leaned forward. "Brian Annetti hurt you?"

She closed her eyes and shook her head. When she reopened them, her gaze fell directly on Enzo. She extended her right arm and pointed her finger at the man who had raped her all those years ago. "No. Not Brian. It was him."

Bree gasped and immediately tried to refocus Ellie. She spoke with a pedantic tone. "That's Enzo, Ellie. You know him."

But none of them could tear away their stares from Ellie's extended arm and unwavering finger pointing directly at Enzo's forehead. Ellie shifted her eyes to Ben. "He hurt me." Her voice wasn't panicked, accusatory, or defensive – she made the statement as though she were stating a simple fact. "He hurt me," she repeated.

Ben turned to Enzo. "Were you at the castle that night, Mr. Kennedy?"

Forever his protector, Bree didn't give Enzo a chance to answer. She put her arm across Enzo's chest, holding him back as though he was in danger of being launched through a car windshield while not wearing a seatbelt.

"I beg your pardon," Bree said indignantly. "You show up here thinking you can throw your weight around just because you are the big FBI guy. Let me remind you that we are here voluntarily. We are here to help Ellie. I'll have you know that Enzo was in the emergency room the night Brian and Patty disappeared. I was with him. He wasn't at the castle, Agent Franklin. He was nowhere near Ellie McAllister either."

Ellie lowered her arm and shifted her gaze from Ben to Enzo, her words now intended for her attacker. "You pulled the white ribbon from my hair. You remember." Her voice grew louder. "It's still down there. It's still down there with those kids." She screamed her final five words: "With our blood on it."

The intensity of the moment reached hysteria when Ellie lunged across the table, flailing her hands toward Enzo's face. Ben tried to grab her but she squirmed through his fingers, managing to get her knees on the table. Although Enzo flung his hands over his face and Bree threw herself in front of her husband, Ellie's index finger dug into Enzo's cheek leaving a scratch deep enough for blood droplets to form in its downward path to his chin.

For the second time, Agent Benjamin Franklin pushed the emergency button in the interrogation room. Officers burst in and restrained Ellie in her chair.

Ben shuffled Bree and Enzo into the lobby. "I need a medic!"

In the hall, Bree surveyed Enzo's neck, pretending not to notice his gauze-wrapped hand. "She's out of control. That woman has lost her mind."

"A medic is on the way."

"Don't bother," Bree huffed, tugging Enzo's collar to follow her out the door.

Chief Walker stepped next to Ben. "I was behind the window listening to the audio. That was sure rough on Enzo. Want us to get the transport ready to the Psych Center?"

Ben needed to think for a moment about what he wanted. "Thanks, but not yet. Can you keep her here in the infirmary?"

Hollis nodded. "Will do. Need anything else?"

Ben thought again about what he needed. "I'd like to see the hospital files for anyone seen in the emergency room on June 20, 1990. Who can I go to for that?"

The chief jotted that down in a small notebook. "I'll head over to the hospital. Dr. Byong, Hyo's father, oversees the hospital's medical records. I'll tell him it's urgent."

"Give him my number," Ben said.

Hollis nodded. "Anything else?"

"What can you tell me about Enzo Kennedy?"

"That you are the second law enforcement officer to ask me that question in the last hour."

"Who else asked about him?" Ben said.

"Agent Ameth Baxter called me about half an hour ago. You know her?"

"Do I ever."

CHAPTER 47

A soft drizzle fell from the dark afternoon clouds rolling in from Canada during the drive from the police station to the Kennedy home. Enzo gripped the steering wheel tightly, repeatedly turning his head from the wet road to Bree who had maintained a steadfast stare out the front windshield. He considered pulling into the parking lot of Castle Wine and Spirits to prevent any drought in Bree's vodka supply but abandoned the idea once he realized he had just one mile to rehearse believable excuses.

Either Enzo had become well-versed in forming convincing justifications for his bad behavior or Bree had become more gullible in believing them. Both Enzo and Bree knew that all his excuses boiled down to one sentiment: *I'm doing this for you.*

With the car parked in the driveway, the couple walked up the back deck stairs and into the kitchen. Bree turned on him, not even bothering to close the door.

"What did Ellie mean that you hurt her?"

Enzo tried to ignore the comment. "Ellie is so much worse than I had expected. She was talking crazy." He went to his wife and held her arms at her sides, but Bree pushed him away.

She rambled through her thoughts. "Ellie said there is a ribbon with your blood on it, with her blood on it, still inside the castle. She said it fell on their bodies. I heard her say that." Bree shook her head. "You hurt her, Enzo. You hurt my friend."

Enzo took a step closer to Bree. "It's not true, and I can't believe you would side with that madwoman. Darling, listen to me."

Never taking her eyes off Enzo, Bree reached to her side and grabbed a round handle of a small drawer, the size that would hold dish towels or hot plate trivets. She pulled it open, never breaking her stare. Bree reached into the drawer and lifted up a handful of colorful ribbons – reds, blues, purples, yellows. She held her hand high and opened her fingers, letting them fall to the floor in a heap. "Since our wedding day, I've saved every ribbon from every flower arrangement you have ever sent me and kept them right here."

"Bree..."

Bree bellowed. "You hurt Ellie!"

"I'm a sinner, Bree. I'm not a perfect man. I'm not a perfect husband." Enzo lifted his chin and pointed at the long scrape on his neck that had already begun to scab. "See this? I deserve to suffer. I deserve this pain," he said, sounding like a pathetic, perverted version of Arthur Dimmesdale flogging himself over his daughter's existence.

Enzo took a step closer to his wife.

Bree cocked her head. "You were there that night," Bree said. "You didn't fall on the dock."

Enzo's deep snarl just inches from Bree's face were muffled by a chipper greeting.

"Hello. Hello," Claudine said, pushing the kitchen door farther open. "I thought I heard voices in here. Is everything okay?" She stepped in, looking at each of them with a hopeful smile. "I hope I didn't interrupt."

Enzo and Bree turned only their heads toward Claudine.

The door was open, they thought in unison. *She heard what we said.*

Enzo went to the sink. Bree turned to the unexpected visitor. "Claudine. What brings you by?"

Did you forget? I can always just meet you at the church."

Bree searched her brain for the reason for Claudine's visit. "The altar," she said. "The movers come tomorrow. Claudine, I had completely forgotten about that."

"What's at the church?" he asked, smiling broadly, all traces of anger now vanished from his face.

Claudine explained. "St. Elizabeth's is closed for repairs. The crew arrives tomorrow to start delivering supplies for the facelift. Father needed a few people from Altar and Rosary Society to pack some things, and we volunteered."

"How nice of you both," Enzo said flatly.

I'll tell you what," Claudine said. "I'm going to run a few errands around town, so I'll join you there in about half an hour. Remember to use the side door." Even though Claudine's words emphasized logistics, her eyes sent Bree a completely different message, an urgent one: *Are you okay? Do you need help?*

Bree read those secret messages, and, using subtle facial cues, she responded by not breaking eye contact with her. It was a soft blink that reassured Claudine that she could leave.

"Perfect," Bree said, but remembered the logistics of the church. "Wait. Do you know the security code? I thought Father said he would email one of us the code, but I don't remember seeing it."

"I have it," Claudine said, tapping her purse.

Bree nodded.

Claudine turned and left, closing the door tightly behind her.

Enzo and Bree listened to their unexpected visitor's footsteps descend to the bottom of the deck stairs before uttering a word.

"She heard us," Enzo said. "She knows."

Bree shook her head. "We can't be sure."

"We *can* be sure. The door was open, Bree." He rubbed his hands with his face, then noticed that his wife's attention had turned to his own hand. He saw that the gauze that had covered his new tattoo had unraveled. Bree lifted his hand to her face to examine the small, black rosary beads etched onto his puffy, glossy skin.

"It's gone? After all these years, you chose to change it today, on the very day the kids were found?"

Enzo saw his opportunity to flip her insinuation. "Nothing I do ever makes you happy, does it?" He shoved the inked rosary against Bree's face. "I did this for you! I got it because I know how much you hated that scar. Hideous, you would call it. That's what you think of me. Admit it!"

Bree stepped away, shaking her head. "No. No. I would never say that about you."

His voice grew louder. "All of this is your fault. I'll be sent away, and you'll be left here all alone. Did you hear me? All of this is your fault!"

Bree shook in frustration and fear, wiping tears from her eyes at the thought of losing the only man she ever loved. "No. No. I'll fix it," Bree said. "I'll fix everything."

CHAPTER 48

Ben listened to his boss in his earpiece while he walked along a cobblestone trail along the river trying to connect the dots.

"Cold case was reviewing the 1995 rape of a Syracuse college student," Baxter said. "Kennedy's name popped up as having a parking ticket a few blocks away from the dorm."

Nut crack.

"The woman who confessed to killing the teens just accused Enzo Kennedy of hurting her," Ben said.

Nut crack.

"Hurting her in what way?"

"She didn't clarify, but she pointed at him before trying to rip his eyes out in the interrogation room."

Nut crack.

"Bring him in for questioning," Baxter said.

"The mental state of the accuser is under serious question right now," Ben said. "They just sedated her, and the plan is to transport her to your neck of the woods for a psych eval."

"You're hesitating," Baxter said. "Why?"

He pushed thoughts of Opal from his mind.

"I screwed up this case once, and I don't want to do that again. Before I charge anyone with anything, I'd like some definitive evidence, some matching DNA, something irrefutably solid."

Nut crack.

"Then go find some."

And the line went dead.

Ben headed toward Alex Bay Park in the center of town, grateful for a patch of billowing clouds to block the glaring sun providing a much-needed respite from the heat. While walking the four blocks on this humid morning, he thought of the Annettis and the Flanagans, wondering if he could have done more, should have done more, to find Brian and Patty. He sank into a wooden park bench, setting his elbows on his knees and resting his chin on his intertwined fingers of flesh and metal. Ben's frustration was palpable as he leaned back on the bench feeling unfocused and lost.

His phone rang and the caller's name filled him with dread. He lifted it to his ear and listened to the young officer's medical update on Luke Annetti's condition. Ben blew the air out of his lungs in relief.

"That's great news," Ben said before repeating Rico's next words. "Yes, thank God for blanks." Ben knew how much damage blanks could inflict on the human body at close range and how lucky Luke Annetti was to have pulled through the procedure performed by top surgeons in the region. "Any idea when he might regain consciousness? I'd like to be the one to tell him about his son and Patty."

Ben listened and learned that the doctors were optimistic about his recovery but are choosing to keep him sedated for a few more days until the brain swelling had reduced by half. Each fact about Luke's recovery eased Ben's guilt, allowing him to focus and remind himself that he needed to do what he did best – observe his surroundings, look for inconsistencies, absorb the details of his environment. He set down his phone and leaned back.

He watched a Pizza Village food truck pull beside the park's wooden gazebo. No sooner did it situate itself than customers lined up at its front window, cash in hand, waiting to be served slices of steaming cheese and pepperoni. A tall, thin man escorted his greyhound east while a short, round woman led her French bulldog west. He saw Claudine Schatz buzz by in her golf cart and park in the paved lot at St. Elizabeth's Church before entering through its north side door. He saw Fiona Wilder exit Margaret's Book and Craft Shop carrying paint brushes and almost get leveled by a group of young skateboarders heading to the beach, towels strung around their necks, most likely looking for a combination of tanning and trouble. A male mime, dressed in black trousers and a striped, black and white shirt, exited his rusty, green sedan, with a cigarette between his lips; he popped open his trunk and took out a hinged placard. Within minutes of flicking his cigarette butt onto the street and setting his sign on the sidewalk, he began juggling five red balls, awaiting pedestrians to start dropping dollar bills into a large empty tin can at his feet.

Juggling. The discovery of the missing teens, Luke Annetti's attempted suicide, Ellie McAllister's confession, Ellie McAllister's accusation, and a parking ticket that could connect Enzo Kennedy to a rape case, Ben felt like he was juggling five different cases in the air. When he added "Opal's rejection" to the mix, the balls fell in different directions. He knew he had to remove her from his mind, that this wasn't the time for any distractions. If he was going to tie up loose ends in this case, it had to be on his own terms with immovable, set parameters. He knew it was the only way.

Ben spotted Hollis in the crosswalk holding up two iced teas with straws. The chief sat beside Ben on the bench. "Here you go. I spotted you from across the street. Thought you could use this since this heat wave won't let up."

"Thanks," Ben said. "Hear anything about those hospital records?"

Hollis shook his head. "Dr. Byong was called to an emergency in the ER, so I left a message on his voicemail about what medical records you wanted, along with your number."

"Thanks for that, Hollis." He reciprocated the favor. "I just hung up with Agent Baxter."

"Why did she want to know about Enzo Kennedy?"

Ben felt his gut tighten, then decided to keep Baxter's information private. He knew that secrets were better kept in big cities than in small towns. He spoke with comfort. "Turned out to be a coincidence."

Hollis slapped his knee. "I'm not surprised at that."

Ben took a sip from his straw, then kept his tone casual. "Why is that?"

"Mr. Kennedy has a long-time legacy for being in the right place at the right time."

"Really? This is the first I've heard about it."

Hollis explained. "About ten years ago, well before my time as police chief, Enzo found a jogger unconscious at the Westcott Beach State Park, north of Syracuse. I was down south then; my dad had told me about the incident."

"He probably called 911?" Ben said, hoping that an audio recording existed.

"Nope. Enzo transported her to Crouse Hospital himself."

"He tampered with the scene," Ben said as innocently as he could.

"The doctors say he saved her life," Hollis said.

Ben detected a hint of defensiveness in Hollis's voice. He forced himself to turn his investigative tone into a conversational one. "What was he doing in Syracuse?"

"Under Mr. Kennedy's direction, ten branches of the Alexandria Bay National Bank have opened around Syracuse and the Thousand Islands region. Back in the day, I hear he used to spend more time in that area than in this one."

Ben raised his eyebrows. "Really? That must have taken a toll on Mrs. Kennedy."

Hollis brushed away the possibility that the Kennedys faced any difficulties in their marriage. "Mrs. Kennedy was everyone's favorite art teacher, so she was always busy with art shows and private classes, that sort of thing."

Ben feigned genuine interest. "Wow. When else was he in the right place at the right time?"

"He confirmed the ID of the man who assaulted a teenage girl on her way home from soccer practice. Enzo had happened to be cutting through the alleyway between the Pirate Motel and Castle Gifts just as she was being attacked."

"The girl couldn't ID the assailant," Ben clarified as he jotted down mental notes.

"She had in earbuds. Never heard him come up behind her," Hollis said. "Enzo said he chased him off and called the police."

"So, they got the guy?" Ben said.

"Yes. Thank God Enzo got a good look at him. Turns out it was the town drunk, Bernie Maxwell, exactly who we expected it to be. Bernie wouldn't be in jail right now if it weren't for Enzo Kennedy's statement and testimony. Some see him as a local hero."

Ben would not tip his hand. "As they should," he said.

Chief Walker tipped his cup forward and Ben tapped it.

"Come on," Hollis said. "It's getting late. Let's go grab some dinner. My treat."

Ben nodded. "I'll take you up on that. Thanks." They stood in unison.

But before they could leave, the mime, attracted the attention of both men by acting out a scenario of him robbing a bank and packing heavy gold bricks into a box that was too heavy to drag to his sedan. His show was convincing and entertaining for both men that they missed Bree Kennedy entering St. Elizabeth's Church through its side door.

CHAPTER 49

The last time Opal Schatz had sat in the Alex Bay waiting room, she had been waiting to learn if her husband was alive or dead. A year later, she was waiting for the same news about her daughter.

After repeatedly pacing between the nurse's station and the elevator, and after stacking the magazines on the side table in chronological order by year and month, Opal decided to check on her staff at *The River Gazette*. She had texted Roxie about Howard and Ruby, asking her if she could put out the morning edition on her own. Once Roxie had confirmed, Opal texted her to use the notes on her desk to write the front-page article.

"I got this. Focus on your family," Roxie texted back.

She was about to text Ben to explain why she couldn't show up at the station to continue questioning Ellie but stopped. *He's busy with the case*, she thought. *I shouldn't bother him with my personal life.*

Hours passed. Opal's faith waned while she watched the red sun set behind Quill Castle out a cloudy hospital window, wondering if the image in front of her symbolized life or death.

Wearing green scrubs, Dr. Jin Byong burst through the door marked *Restricted Area* and removed his mask. He went right to Opal and grabbed her shoulders. "They're going to be okay."

Opal collapsed into his arms, her howling sobs releasing waves of pent-up worry. "Oh, thank God."

"What happened? Was it food poisoning?" Opal asked.

Jin cocked his head. "More like a poisoning of their food."

Opal felt her head spin and instinctively sat back down.

"There were no Staphylococcus bacteria present in either Ruby or Howard, so traditional food poisoning was ruled out. After we got those results, I ordered a basophilic stippling on the peripheral smear. That test came back positive for high levels of arsenic."

Opal laughed in disbelief. "Arsenic?"

Jin nodded. "I heard the EMTs had bagged an unopened jar of peaches at the scene and sent it to the police lab for testing. The Chief said he would call when the results were in."

Opal let go of trying to make sense of a bizarre set of circumstances. "When can I see her? When can I see them?"

Jin shook his head. "Soon but not yet. They should start waking up on their own in the morning. Take some time. Go home. Catch a nap. Shower. Change. She isn't alone. Hyo hasn't left Ruby's side. Your daughter is special to my daughter."

"Our girls are very much in love," Opal said. "Thank you, doc. I'll be back first thing in the morning."

At home, Opal slept like the dead.

CHAPTER 50

Lavender and menthol-laced bubbles floated in the pink plastic basin on the bedside table. His sponge bath was over.

Miss Rosa helped Mr. Xavier ease his arms into his robe. She squeezed out the sponge and gathered together the towels she had used to dry his skin. "I tried being gentle when I dried your back, so I hope it didn't hurt when I patted those marks. Are they scars?"

He shook his head. "They appeared when I was in my teens. Unfortunately, my grandfather saw them as an omen."

Rosa clucked her tongue. "That's silly. I'll tell you what: they are nature's tattoos and quite beautiful."

"Certainly better than my relationship with my grandfather," he quipped, before his grin faded. "Can I ask you something?"

She sat on the corner of the bed, waiting for the question. "Of course."

"Do people know when they are going to die?"

She touched his hand. "Sometimes."

He thought about her answer. "When death is close, what do they wish for?"

Rosa had become comfortable talking about death, a skill that had proven itself both helpful and hurtful with patients and their families. "To see the people they love," she said. "Both past and present."

He nodded. "I have information to share before I die."

"Would you like me to contact your family?"

His cauled eye lolled toward her. "There is no one to call. I will die alone through no fault of anyone else."

Rosa touched his shoulder. "Anything you say to me regarding transferring your possessions would not be legally binding."

"I want to end the curse on my family line," he said. "I just need something delivered to someone."

"We have a legal department who works with Manor Oak in cases like this," she said. "I can contact them on your behalf."

He shook his head. "There's no time. I need this done before I die." His voice grew weary.

Rosa removed her hand from his shoulder, but he grabbed her arm with such force, her breath caught in her throat.

He pulled her close. "There is no time. Please. I'm asking you to deliver something while I'm still alive. No lawyers are needed to oversee a simple courier delivery."

She considered his logic and nodded.

He patted the side of the bed. She sat and listened to his story, to his wish. His voice softened in sorrow and rose with urgency as he told the details of his tale. When he finished, he looked at her through wet eyes.

She exhaled a deep breath, considered his request, then set her hand onto his. "Yes. I can do that."

"Today?" he asked.

"Today," she said.

CHAPTER 51

Ben awoke the next morning at the Bijou House and felt good. He hadn't slept that soundly in years, since before Gail got sick. He hummed a few bars of John Philip Sousa's "Stars and Stripes Forever" as he descended the staircase to a banquet-sized room for breakfast. Grabbing a couple of mini-muffins, he stuffed them into his mouth then pulled the carafe lever forward to fill a paper to-go cup with coffee. He sipped on the hot coffee to wash them down. His airiness evaporated in an instant when he turned to leave. The once delightful and gracious hosts, the Ladendorfs, who had just days ago shared the entire story of how the Thousand Islands House became the Bijou House and how they worked tirelessly to acquire the property, stood in front of the door with their arms folded across their chests and deep scowls on their faces.

Ben had to ask. "Mr. and Mrs. Ladendorf. Is something wrong?"

"Is it true?" Mrs. Ladendorf asked, stepping toward him.

"Is what true?" Ben said.

The couple rolled their eyes in deep disgust.

"That the FBI could have found those poor teens' bodies years ago if they hadn't ignored evidence mailed to the newspaper right here in Alex Bay," she said. Mr. Ladendorf held out the morning's edition of *The River Gazette*. "Who's DNA is it, anyway?"

In disbelief, Ben read and reread the extra-large headline splashed across the front page.

Flawed FBI: Agent Ignored Evidence in Missing Teens Case

Ben snatched the paper and read the four-column article that detailed – often verbatim – the off-the-record information he had told Opal over breakfast. To make matters worse, the article surrounded a large rectangular photo of himself standing on Starr Island, a photo Roxie must have taken the night he arrived on the scene. He was back in the limelight again. *Son of a bitch.*

He gave the newspaper back and spoke definitively. "I'll be checking out tomorrow morning. Thank you for your hospitality. The Bijou House is a lovely place to stay." Ben walked out the front door and down the stone path toward his car in the lot. A thick mixture of fury and betrayal pick-axed its way into his heart. *How could I have been so stupid?* he thought, emphasizing the last word.

Ben didn't need to look at caller ID to know that Ameth Baxter was on the other end of his ringing phone. He wanted to get in the first word. "I'm just as surprised as you. That information was absolutely off the record."

And to Ben's surprise, Ameth didn't reprimand him for breaking strict protocols by sharing confidential information with the town's primary media outlet. She didn't even crack a pistachio into the receiver. When Ameth finally spoke, she didn't tip her hand. "I'd like you to come in for a meeting at noon. See you then." That was it. The line went dead.

"Shit."

How could I have been so stupid? he thought again, this time emphasizing the first word. He climbed inside his car, and instead of turning right and jumping on I-81S toward Syracuse, he turned left to confront that manipulative editor of *The River Gazette*.

CHAPTER 52

Rested and showered, Opal left her house for the hospital before her morning newspaper was delivered to her porch.

Jin was waiting for her at the nurse's station with good news. "Howard and Ruby had productive nights. I'm keeping them sedated until this afternoon so their organs can recover."

"Can I see them?"

"In a few minutes. The nurses are in with them now."

Opal nodded.

Assuming she knew about her daughter's pregnancy, Jin said, "I wonder when they'll make the announcement."

"About what?" Opal said.

Jin hesitated, dodging the question as best he could. "I just thought they were getting close to taking the big step," he lied.

"A wedding? They're getting married?" Opal couldn't hold in a squeal in delight.

"No, no, no," Jin said. "I don't know for sure. I guess I just have a feeling."

"I've always wanted to help plan her wedding, but I sort of gave up on that when she entered her forties. She knows I'll want to run an engagement photo in the paper," she said.

He tried to use her reference to dig himself out of the hole he had swiftly dug. "Speaking of the paper, the article about the FBI dropping the ball was quite shocking."

Opal didn't understand his point. "What?"

Jin grabbed a folded newspaper at the nurse's station and handed it to her. "It's just unbelievable that the FBI found the same DNA on those letters. It must belong to Ellie since she confessed, right? The case against her will be open and shut." He looked at his buzzing pager. "The nurse will let you know when you can go back to see them." He hustled away through the doors, returning to the restricted zone.

Opal didn't hear a word he said because she was staring at a headline that she knew shouldn't exist.

"No. No. No. No. No. No. This is impossible," she said, crumpling the paper to her chest. She extended her arms again and reread it.

"Shit."

Not wanting to waste a second getting to her office, she bypassed the elevator and took the stairs.

CHAPTER 53

Opal was out of breath from running the four blocks from the hospital to her office but huffed out a "What the hell happened?" and dropped the morning edition on Roxie's desk.

Roxie frowned. She had been expecting a congratulatory pat on the back, not a reprimand. She gave her only defense. "You told me to write the story."

"You used the wrong notes." Opal set her palm against her cheek, entirely covering her birthmark, closed her eyes and repeated herself. "You used the wrong notes!"

Roxie stood. "You said to use the notes *in* your desk when you texted me from the hospital."

Her eyes flicked open. "I said *on* my desk," Opal said.

"No. you said *in* your desk. Look." Roxie held up her phone, showing Opal their text history.

A knot tightened in Opal's stomach as she read her own words. "I made a mistake. The notes on my desk were fair game. The ones you used, the ones that were in my desk, were strictly off-the-record. I promised Ben, I mean, I promised Agent Franklin, that I wouldn't use his comments. I gave him my word."

Roxie understood the seriousness of the moment. "I could have double-checked."

"It's not your fault." Opal released a long sigh. "It's squarely mine."

"Fucking prepositions," Roxie said.

"The strain of learning about Howard and Ruby," Opal began. "I wasn't thinking clearly. He'll need to understand."

Roxie nodded. "He knows about Howard and Ruby?"

Opal shook her head. "No. I haven't seen him yet to tell him. All that matters right now is that they are going to be okay. The rest will work itself out." She noticed a change in Roxie's expression. Her smile seemed frozen on her face. "Why do you look like a happy mannequin?"

"First, let me tell you that Ebony White keeps calling here," Roxie said. "She asked why you're not returning her calls or texts."

"Because I'm ignoring her. I have too much on my plate."

"That's an understatement," Roxie said.

"What else do you have to tell me?"

"Agent Franklin is in your office."

Opal glanced toward the closed door and back to her reporter. "He's in there right now?"

Roxie nodded. "He arrived a few minutes before you. He's hoppin' mad."

Opal nibbled on the nail of her index finger before forming a fist and jamming it on her hip. "He'll just have to understand. Mistakes happen."

Standing outside her office, Opal raised her chin and stepped inside, closing the door behind her softly. She took quick steps to her chair and sat down at her desk. With half-raised eyes, she could see Ben sitting in a wooden chair, legs crossed, with one foot jostling up and down.

She folded her hands neatly on the desk before lifting her gaze to meet his. "I'm sorry. I never meant for anyone to see what you told me privately. Turns out, I had sent Roxie a text when I was at the…"

Ben snorted. "The reason really doesn't matter. We had an agreement. You broke it. I trusted you," he said sharply. "Now, the FBI and the person leading the investigation – namely me – look like a bunch of inexperienced knuckleheads."

Opal swallowed hard. "I can explain."

Ben mentally pulled up a transcript of their conversation at the café and recited it back to her as though he were a court reporter ordered by a judge to read back testimony: "I give you, my word."

Opal cringed in shame.

Ben uncrossed his legs and leaned forward. "Not only that, but I just got called back to the regional office. They're probably taking me off the case."

Opal's eyes went wide in protest. "No. They can't do that. This is your case!"

Ben stood up. "You listen to me, Mrs. Schatz. You are not to have any further contact or involvement with this case or with any aspect of the investigation. You will not visit the crime scene looking for any additional evidence."

Opal cocked her head. "Do you think there is something else to find at the crime scene?"

Ben saw the challenge in her eyes and ignored her question, continuing to bark a litany of restrictions and orders at her. "You will not launch speculative theories," he said, adjusting his belt buckle. "You will let the FBI investigate, and you will receive the findings when they are officially released just like everyone else."

Opal tried to interrupt. "Please, Ben. I can explain if you give me a chance."

"There are no second chances with this one," he said. "Stay out of my case and stay away from the castle."

And as Opal tried to tell Ben that Ruby and Howard were poisoned, that she stayed at the hospital all night wondering if her daughter would live or die, Ben turned on his heel and walked out the door.

CHAPTER 54

Jin stepped into a stairwell and climbed up two floors to the hospital lab, a white-walled room filled with microscopes, centrifuges, and test tubes. He glanced around, uncertain of where to find someone for an updated toxicology report. His go-to tech, Bruce, a large balding bulk of a man who shared his love of stuffed banana peppers, wasn't in his usual spot perched on a stool looking into a microscope. The long lab table, typically surrounded by bustling pathologists, lay vacant.

He walked down a long corridor and spotted what looked like a staff meeting in a windowed room. Staff members in white lab jackets listened intently to someone speaking at the front of the room. From his angle, he couldn't see who was holding their attention.

A sudden whiff of bleach made him wince and rub his nose. He turned and saw a maintenance woman mopping the floor near a water fountain. Once he passed her by, he could see who kept the attention of the pathology department.

Jin peeked his head into the private meeting and addressed the speaker directly. "Chief Walker. Do you have news to share about the Case of the Poisoned Peaches?"

"Hi, Doc," Hollis said. "I was just thanking the staff for contacting the department about the evidence collected at the scene."

"What did they find?" he said, looking at him and then to the seated staff.

"You know already that the EMTs bagged a mostly eaten peach pie, a tin, and plastic forks from a garbage can in Howard's office at Manor Oak, but they also brought in a jar of unopened peaches from Howard's desk. Both items had handwritten labels stating that Claudine Schatz made them. The correct protocol was followed in contacting my department. We're bringing her in for questioning."

"Claudine?" Jin said, sitting in an open chair. He rubbed his temple with his index finger. "Why on Earth would Claudine purposely harm her husband and niece?"

CHAPTER 55

Wearing a knee-length, cornflower blue cotton dress, Claudine felt smug. With her plan to avenge her reputation in the works, she grinned in delight. She was not about to sit back and look the other way, to simply forgive and be the better person. Not this time. Not with her tramp sister-in-law still polluting her family line. Bree would be her alibi. "Yes, members of the jury. Claudine Schatz volunteered in a church the day Opal's body was found. She seemed entirely herself."

Once through the side door of St. Elizabeth's Church, Claudine typed in the security code on a square pad of numbers beside a stained-glass window. She waited until the small red light turned green before flicking on the church lights to assess the progress made by the packing team a day earlier. Twenty large cardboard boxes, each marked with a home improvement store's logo, had already been sealed and stacked neatly along the wall leading to the vestibule. She nodded, satisfied. "That's a start," she said to the boxes.

Father Dominic's decision to visit Italy couldn't have come at a worse time. The long-awaited capital project to repair broken pews, install a wheelchair elevator, and expand the altar had been planned for over a year. A frantic call from his sister in Cicero telling him that she refused to become a grandmother if his niece wasn't properly married led him to purchase a plane ticket that day. In just two days, he had organized groups of volunteers to pack items for storage and had moved church services to St. Gregory's for the three weeks he would be gone. Although his sister thought he booked the trip solely to marry off her daughter, he planned to spend time with his niece to explore the meaning of love, to ask how she felt about her boyfriend and the baby. If his sister found that unacceptable, he knew he might find himself back on American soil sooner than later.

Looking around the altar, Claudine quickly deduced that Father had selected Bree and her, the two longest-serving Society members, to properly pack the most sacred items used by the celebrant during masses, namely, the chalice that held the blood of Christ and the Tabernacle, which protected His body. Father must have thought they deserved the honor.

The third item he left for them to pack was none other than the dagger Claudine had once thought she owned. It sat behind a clear fiberglass structure, similar to the one that she had installed in her home. She reached up, popped the latch, and grabbed the dagger by its handle; she drew it up close to her face to admire its rubies and emeralds glisten and twinkle in the soft lighting. A small tag dangling from a white string rested in the palm of her hand.

#71706070528
Property of the Metropolitan Museum of Art

It wasn't the serial number that triggered a few drops of urine to leak from her bladder. It was the next two words – *property of* – that tensed her bladder. The tag. A label. Her label. *From Claudine's Kitchen.* Sweat formed on her neck. She had to force herself to suck in deep breaths of air through her nose, expelling it out her mouth.

Always her last step in the canning process, she had written those words hundreds of times before submitting her jams, jellies, and pies to Jefferson County Fair officials. And now she saw her mistake, one she committed mostly out of habit, one that would lead the police to her front door. *The best-laid plans of mice and men often go awry*, she thought.

"Hello, Claudine," Bree said.

Claudine whirled around, pointing the dagger at her.

"Whoa," Bree said, holding up her hands. "Take it easy."

Realizing how she looked, Claudine laughed at herself, setting the dagger on a box. "Sorry. I just wanted to have another look at it."

Bree went to her and picked up the knife. "It *is* quite beautiful." She examined the jewels and eyed its silver blade.

Claudine gave Bree the once-over from head to toe. "You're wearing black. I don't think I've ever seen you wear black. Long sleeves and pants in this heat?" she asked.

Bree slid the small nylon cinch sack off her back, the one Enzo had packed for her, the one he had insisted she took with her to confront Claudine.

She ignored Claudine's comment. "I need to ask you what you heard Enzo and me discussing earlier. You know, when you were on the deck listening."

Claudine shook her head. "No. I didn't mean to. The door was open. Then I heard you shouting."

"So, you heard," Bree said. "You know everything."

Claudine nodded, opening her purse and taking out her phone. "When we go to the police, we can show them this." She tilted her phone toward Bree, revealing the photo she had snapped from Jin's desk in the medical records office.

Bree frowned. "How did you get this?"

And in a moment of pure selflessness, Claudine forgot about the poisoned pie, forgot about a court case that would likely show patterns against her. For the first time, she put someone else first. "It doesn't matter how. Just read it. The doctor had written that he thought Enzo's injury was the result of a human bite mark. We can tell the police to match the photo to his dental records."

Bree shook her head.

Undeterred in her insistence, Claudine stepped closer to her friend. "Yes. I can give the police a statement about what I heard on the deck, and you can confirm it. We can show this to Ellie."

Bree's grip on the dagger tightened. "Conversations between a husband and wife are privileged, so what you heard will be considered hearsay and inadmissible. Besides, during the interrogation this morning, Ellie said there was blood evidence still in the castle."

Claudine set her hands on Bree's shoulders. "That's even better! When they find the physical evidence we tell them about, Enzo will be put away for good. You'll be free of him." With that, the Peach Pie County Champion smiled proudly. "Blood doesn't lie."

"Exactly," Bree said, plunging the dagger into Claudine's abdomen at an upward angle, instantly piercing a lung.

A gurgling moan escaped Claudine's lips before her head fell forward onto Bree's shoulder. She jerked upright, staring into the eyes of a woman she had considered her friend for over six decades.

Bree whispered to her: "You won't take my husband from me."

Adrenaline and panic seized Claudine; her body instinctively tried to escape by stumbling forward toward the wooden pews, but her attempt to flee fell short when she tumbled through the purple curtain and into the confessional. Only the blue hem of her dress, already soaked in drops of blood, and her bloodied knee, remained visible outside the curtain. After just a moment more of movement, her knee rested still against the mahogany molding.

Bree needed time to think. She peeked inside the booth to see Claudine's vacant eyes staring back at her, the dagger still solidly in place. Using her foot, she tapped Claudine's knee. No movement. She backed away, crossing the altar to Father Dominic's chair, which sat under a life-sized Jesus hanging on an even larger cross. Bree collapsed on the cushion, then jumped at the ring of her phone.

She was about to dismiss the call with her bloody hand when she recognized the familiar number. Tapping the call button, she listened to Opal's simple request. "Can you make some time for your bestie?"

Bree sucked in a deep breath and spoke in a friendly, conversational tone. "For you, girl, anything. Wait – first tell me about Ruby? I've been worried sick."

"She's going to be okay. They don't know how but both Howard and Ruby have high levels of arsenic in their systems. By the grace of God, they were saved."

"Arsenic! My God, Opal," Bree said, thinking of how to bait her long-time friend. "I don't want to add to your worries right now."

"What do you mean? Has something happened?"

Bree grinned. "I don't want to bother you about how the questioning went with Ellie."

"Tell me!"

Bree smiled for two reasons. First, she didn't have to use the gun in her backpack to kill Claudine; she had feared the bang would have attracted attention. Secondly, Opal's trust was unwavering, making it easier than she had thought to reduce her to a mere pawn against a mighty queen.

"It was terrible," Bree said, faking a voice of distress. "Ellie was screaming and saying wild things. She said a man attacked her that night, that there is still evidence – his blood on a hair ribbon – at the bottom of the chamber where the kids were found. Ellie said that blood will lead to the real killer's identity and clear her name."

Opal's words murmured frustration. "How could she not have told anyone?"

"She said that the man hurt her, Opal."

Bree waited for the words to further unsettle her friend before setting the hook. "I was going to see if Mac would take me out there, but I don't know the castle like you do. I wouldn't know where to begin," Bree said. "They are going to move Ellie to a psych ward for an evaluation in a few hours. I wanted to at least *try* to save her."

Ben's voice suddenly popped into Opal's head: *You listen to me, Mrs. Schatz. You are not to have any further contact or involvement with this case or with any aspect of the investigation. You will not visit the crime scene looking for any additional evidence.*

Opal arched an eyebrow. "Meet me at the dock in ten minutes. We're going to help our friend."

CHAPTER 56

Summer held on to its last vibrant colors of the day as Opal maneuvered *My Gem IV* near the Quill Castle's dock so that Bree could secure a braided rope around a beam. Opal left the keys in the ignition. "I'm leaving them here, so I don't drop them in there."

Bree nodded, swinging a small knapsack around her shoulders. "We know what we're looking for. It shouldn't take long. Lead the way."

The bright lights atop wooden poles allowed them to follow the same trail Brian Annetti and Patty Flanagan had followed twenty-five years ago. Once the women slipped into the kitchen, they flicked on the lights and grabbed the flashlights left on the table by federal agents earlier in the week. The two friends climbed the grand staircase toward the gift shop.

"What exactly did Ellie say was still down there?" Opal asked.

"A hair ribbon, a white one stained with the blood of her assailant."

"And finding it might set Ellie free," Opal said.

Inside the secret room, the women stood on the edge of the broken floorboards, shining their lights into the dark hole, trying to recognize or locate anything that resembled a ribbon.

"It's too far. I can't see much," Bree said.

Opal moaned. "Same here. We need to use something to poke around down there."

In unison, they turned, shining their flashlights around the room and onto a bucket holding long metal scaffolding poles. They went to it and snapped together six of them.

"This should reach the bottom," Opal said, dragging the extension rod across the floor.

"Wait," Bree said. She grabbed the carabiner hook and attached it to the end. "This will clasp onto anything we want to bring to the surface."

Opal lowered the pole, then manned its movement from Bree's directions.

"To the right. Yes. Can you push that board over a little? Good." Bree directed her light from left to right, trying to spot a ribbon stained with her husband's blood. "Wait! Go back," she ordered.

"What do you see?"

"Under that wooden beam, I see some fabric. Pink maybe. Can you catch the end of it with the clip?" Bree said.

Opal leaned forward. "Where? Point to it."

Bree pointed. "There. By that broken board."

"Gotcha," Opal said. "Let me know if I snag it." She maneuvered the pole over and up. On her fourth attempt, the tip of the hook caught a strand of fabric.

"You've got it!" Bree cried. "Careful. Careful now."

Opal took slow steps backward until the end of the pole reached them. Bree reached and grabbed the found treasure.

Opal dropped the pole back into the floor opening and moved her flashlight to their find. The women exchanged a confused glance.

Bree held it up. "This is not a ribbon. It's a pink apron. With daisies."

Opal took it, peering at the pattern. "And blood stains. Could Ellie have thought the apron ties were ribbons? You said she was talking crazy during the interrogation."

Bree's mind raced. *This was a problem. Ellie had seemed so certain that Enzo hurt her in the castle on the night the teens disappeared. But could Ellie have gotten some details wrong? Was she nothing more than an Ophelia in her final hours?*

Bree looked at Opal and nodded confidently, deciding that, yes, she had found what she was looking for. "This must be what she had meant."

"Let's take this to Hollis. He won't be thrilled that we visited the crime scene, but he'll be happy we found some evidence," Opal said, nodding at the apron.

Bree frowned. "Let me have that. I'll put it in my knapsack."

Opal gave the apron to Bree. "Let's go. We can try to catch the chief at the station."

Bree turned to face Opal.

"Sorry, love. We are going to do nothing of the sort."

CHAPTER 57

It took Opal's mind a minute to register that the gun in Bree's hand was real. "What the hell, Bree? Why do you have a gun?"

Bree's voice was deep and cold, the likes of which Opal had never heard before. "I'll tell you what's going on. After we agreed to meet at the dock, I received a call from Enzo. Federal agents arrived at the house to arrest him."

"To arrest Enzo?"

"Turns out they were following the orders of the one and only, Agent Benjamin Franklin."

"But why? For what crime?"

Bree forced herself to say the reason. "The rape of Ellie McAllister."

Opal raised an eyebrow. "That doesn't make any sense. Ben must have made a mistake. That evidence will prove it *wasn't* Enzo," she said nodding at her friend's bag.

"I lied," Bree said.

"I don't understand." The tension between them forced Opal to absorb the reality of the situation: *No one knows I'm here. I left the keys on the boat.*

Bree didn't back down. "The tests will show that the blood on the apron belongs to my husband."

Opal struggled to process Bree's words in a way that would support her understanding of Enzo being a valued family friend. "You're saying that the apron would *free* Ellie and *convict* Enzo?"

Bree nodded. "But no one will ever find out about this pink apron."

Opal blurted out a laugh. "We have to tell the police, Bree. We have no choice."

"We all have choices we are forced to live with," Bree said, taking a step closer to Opal while keeping the tip of the gun aimed at Opal's chest. "No one is going to take my husband away from me."

"Put that gun down, Bree! You're scaring me." Opal softened her voice from anger to sympathy. "Please, Bree. Talk to me."

Bree didn't hesitate. She simply pulled the trigger.

CHAPTER 58

The explosion of pain in Opal's shoulder pushed her backward a few steps to the rim of the broken floorboards, her heels teetering above the depth of nothingness. When she clutched her bloody shoulder, her weight shifted, sending her further backward toward the vacant shaft.

"No!" Opal shouted, realizing that Brian and Patty's final resting place was about to become her grave. When survival mode kicked in, she reached out and grabbed the metal scaffolding propped on the side of the hole, hoping her last effort would ease the brunt of her fall.

She was wrong.

Opal screamed when her hip rammed into metal bolts, crunching her pelvis. She screamed when her scarlet patch of skin slid down a wooden beam, driving thick, sharp slivers into her face. She screamed when she hit the bottom, her ankle bone snapping in two, the force of the fall lurching the bone's jagged tip through her skin from the inside out. For the third time in twenty-five years, an innocent victim lay at the bottom of an abandoned shaft in a heap, broken and bleeding. She knew that she was finished, that she was inching toward death, that this was the end. And that was the moment all went black.

CHAPTER 59

An hour after leaving Alex Bay for Baxter's meeting, Agent Benjamin T. Franklin wasn't any calmer. An equal mix of anger and disappointment festered in his mind as he passed the Watertown exit on Interstate 81S toward Syracuse. Simply put, he had been snookered into revealing confidential information – to a newspaper editor, nonetheless. *Idiot. Idiot. Idiot,* he thought. *It might not have been my first rodeo, but it will certainly be my last.*

His phone rang. He tapped his Bluetooth button and kept pace with his lane of traffic.

"Agent Franklin?" the voice said.

"Yes. This is Ben Franklin."

"I'm Dr. Jin Byong from medical records department at Alexandria Bay Hospital. I received a message from Chief Walker stating that you wanted records for anyone who visited the ER on June 20, 1990."

"Yes. That's right."

"I have the file right here. What exactly did you want to know?" Jin asked.

"What time did Enzo Kennedy check into the ER that night?

A guffaw escaped Jin's lips. "He didn't."

Ben frowned. "Forgive me, Dr. Byong, but I've been told by several sources that you stitched up his hand on the evening Brian Annetti and Patty Flanagan disappeared."

Jin hummed a note. "I can explain the discrepancy," the doctor said. "Enzo arrived at the ER at 12:45 a.m. on June 21, 1990, the day that would have been Brian Annetti's and Patty Flanagan's graduation day. I have it right here. His wife, Bree, brought him in."

Ben thought back to his original notes – Enzo said he didn't check on Ellie when Mac was out of town because he was in the ER getting stitches after a fall on the dock. He was certain he had heard that same explanation from both Mac and Bree. In fact, Ben even remembered his interview with Mac twenty-five years ago had begun with Enzo holding up his injured hand wrapped in tape and gauze. At the time, there was simply no reason to scrutinize his story. Ben clicked on his turn signal and pulled over onto the shoulder. He shifted his vehicle into park.

Ben's mind raced. *Technically, Enzo Kennedy doesn't have an alibi for his whereabouts the night the kids disappeared*, he thought. *But Ellie already confessed to the crime. What am I missing?* "I know it was a long time ago, Dr. Byong, but do you remember anything unusual about Enzo Kennedy's visit to the ER that morning?"

"I remember it was a wild night. People still talk about that day."

"Why is that?" Ben wedged his left elbow onto the door's window and rubbed his index finger into his temple. He closed his eyes as he listened.

"Well, first, it was the night of the Alex Bay Carnival," Jin said. "The ER usually fills up quickly with kids who fall when running from ride to ride along with adults who spent all day in the beer tent. The rain certainly didn't help. The ER was bursting at the seams," he said. "But secondly, the school board meeting ran late that night."

Ben didn't follow. "I'm sorry, doctor. I don't see what one has to do with the other."

Jin chuckled. "That's because you're not from around here." He started at the beginning. "Each year on graduation eve, the Board of Education holds its final meeting of the school year on the football field at five o'clock to certify the diplomas of the graduates by ringing the school bell. Once that bell rings, everyone heads down to Alex Bay Park for a carnival to honor the soon-to-be graduates. You know, everyone enjoys midway rides and food vendors. It's a tradition. But that night, the meeting ran very late."

Ben hoped the story would move along. "Why is that?"

"Someone had stolen the bell."

Ben grinned. "Really."

"The principal at the time, Carl Bixby, refused to certify the results until the bell was returned to its proper place."

Ben opened his eyes. "Did they find it?"

"Eventually. But not until much later that night."

"Where was it?" Ben asked, suddenly amused.

"At the bottom of Carl Bixby's in-ground swimming pool."

Ben let out a quick laugh. "So, it would be fair to conclude that Enzo Kennedy didn't get home until late that evening."

Jin corrected him. "Agent Franklin, I can only speak about Bree Kennedy's whereabouts that evening."

"Sorry?" Ben said.

"The person voted favorite teacher is the person who rings the bell and Bree Kennedy didn't do that until almost nine o'clock. Enzo could have been with her or he could have been traveling back from Syracuse that night," Jin said. "Back then, he spent most of his week at other bank branches and returned home on Fridays."

"Does your report have any notes about his whereabouts before he arrived at 12:45?"

"No. I just wrote that the victim's wife brought him in after she arrived home and found her husband bleeding profusely from his hand. He claimed that he had fallen on the dock."

"Claimed?" Ben said. "Did you have reason to think otherwise?"

Dr. Byong snorted a laugh. "Yes, both he and his wife insisted the injury resulted from a fall on a slippery dock."

"And you found that odd?"

"I did. That type of fall wouldn't have resulted in that type of gash. When I took an instant photo of the injury for his file, Mrs. Kennedy became irate, screaming that I didn't have the right to take the picture. A plastic surgeon took him into surgery shortly after that."

"And you found her reaction odd?"

"I did," Jin said.

"Why is that?"

"Because the injury Enzo Kennedy sustained was clearly a bite mark."

Ben sat up straight. "Something bit Enzo Kennedy the night Patty Flanagan and Brian Annetti disappeared?"

"Not something," the doctor clarified. "Someone."

In Ben's mind, the neat, linear timeline of events that had been set in stone for decades dissolved. "Would you text me the photo?" Ben asked.

"Yes, of course. I'll send it now."

"I appreciate that, doc," Ben said, about to end the call. "I'll let you know if I need anything else."

"Wait! Agent Franklin?"

"Yes?"

"After the article in today's paper, I doubt you will be contacting Opal anytime soon, but I'm worried that she hasn't returned any of my calls today. If you happen to see her, could you tell her she can visit Howard and Ruby in the ICU in about an hour?"

Ben frowned. "Why are they in the hospital?"

"I thought you would have heard by now. A maintenance man found them unconscious at Manor Oak last night. They were in bad shape suffering from arsenic poisoning but are going to be okay. Opal paced the hospital halls all night until I ordered her home this morning to get some rest."

Ben rubbed his hands over his face. He instantly recalled his last words to her: *There are no second chances with this one. Stay out of my case.* "So she wasn't in her office last night. Someone else must have put out the paper."

"I would expect so," Jin said.

"When was the last time you spoke with her?" Ben said.

"About four o'clock this morning."

"I spoke to her around nine." Ben's thoughts turned back to Ruby and Howard. "Who would poison them?"

Jin had an answer. "All I know is that Chief Walker is trying to locate Claudine Schatz who now seems to be missing.

I saw Claudine go into the side door of the church, Ben remembered.

"Thanks, doc. I'll text the chief."

The moment he ended the call, Ben typed and sent the message to Hollis about seeing Claudine enter the church through its north side door. But before he could violate the No U-Turn sign by crossing over the grassy median to head north, his phone beeped with a text notification. He tapped the icon and found himself staring at Enzo Kennedy's bloodied hand that clearly showed six short maroon dashes forming an arch into his flesh.

"Jesus Christ," Ben said in disbelief.

He had seen this type of injury before, most often in post-mortem photographs of a serial killer's victim. In those cases, dentists were often called to the stand to match incisor and cuspid indentations to suspects' teeth. Ben spoke as though he were on a witness stand giving testimony: "That wound was not consistent with a fall on a dock. It was, without a doubt, inflicted by another human being."

CHAPTER 60

Ten minutes after reading Agent Franklin's text message, Hollis Walker pushed open the unlocked side door of St. Elizabeth's Church just as its steeple bells jingled out "Faith of our Fathers" during the lunch rush.

He flicked on the lights, half-expecting to see Ellie McAllister sitting in the center pew reciting the rosary, but he knew she had just arrived at a psychiatric facility a hundred miles south across the street from FBI Headquarters in Syracuse.

It was after he passed the packing boxes that were stacked against the side wall of the sacristy that he saw the blood. Lots of it. He clicked on his shoulder intercom. "I need back up at St. Elizabeth's now. No sirens. Side entrance."

With his eyes, Ben traced the trail of blood from the altar to the pews to the confessional before landing them on a blood-stained knee protruding out from a velvet curtain. The dress hem told him the victim wore a cornflower blue dress. Ben moved his hand to his pistol. "This is the police," he called. The knee didn't move.

He repeated himself, louder this time. Still no movement. Hollis stepped toward the confessional and grabbed the right edge of the curtain, sliding it left. The dead body of Claudine Schatz was seated on an interior wooden bench, her back slumped in the corner. Her eyes mirrored Hollis Walker's – wide open, staring at the bedazzled dagger wedged into her chest.

With his right hand, he made the sign of the cross from his forehead to shoulders, offering a blessing to Claudine's soul. He clicked his intercom button again. "I need an ambulance at St. Elizabeth's. And the coroner."

CHAPTER 61

Over the Bluetooth connection, Chief Hollis Walker heard the shock in Ben's voice. "Claudine Schatz is dead?"

"With a nine-inch jeweled, Celtic dagger embedded in her chest in St. Elizabeth's confessional," the chief added.

Ben read the green Thousand Islands exit sign and followed its arrow to the right. "Not the dagger that she had been hanging in the church, the one she had found at the estate sale."

"The one and only. All hell has broken loose since your crew arrested Enzo who has already lawyered up."

"We had expected that," Ben said. "I just got off the exit."

Hollis's voice was focused. "Don't expect to be met with any fanfare after that article in the paper today. Was it Enzo's DNA under the envelopes?"

"As soon as I get confirmation, I'll send you the report," he said. "Hollis, what did the search warrants produce?"

"A hidden compartment in the back of his front desk drawer at the bank. My guys almost missed it."

"What was in it?" Ben said.

Hollis cleared his throat. "A stack of complaint forms against him from women. The earliest one is dated 1995. Their narratives were strikingly similar. Enzo would brush against them when putting away files near a teller at her station. Or, he would stumble into a group of women, always managing to accidentally graze a breast before regaining his balance. Every complaint said that he apologized profusely for his accidental escapades, saying that he was to blame. If you can believe it, in the nineties Enzo rewrote the Bank's sexual harassment protocols so that all complaints had to filter through his office before continuing up the chain to corporate."

"Of course, he did," Ben said, shaking his head. He parked in the marina lot, glad to see Henry washing a small fiberglass skiff in the shallow water outside the boathouse.

"I have to admit that I've been replaying your interrogation of Ellie when Bree and Enzo were in the room," Hollis said. "Did you notice that Bree wouldn't let her husband speak for himself, that she became unhinged when Ellie accused Enzo of hurting her? If Bree had never suspected Enzo of wrongdoing, why was she so defensive?"

Ben updated him on what he had learned. "Dr. Byong got back to me from medical records," Ben said. "He sent me the photo of Enzo's injury. I knew the moment I saw it that someone had bit his hand."

A low groan slipped from Hollis's mouth. "Ellie McAllister fought back."

Silence fell between them.

"We have another problem," Hollis said.

"We can't find Bree or Opal."

Ben held his breath.

Hollis continued. "When did you speak with Opal last? What did she say?"

Ben recalled the conversation. "I talked with her at nine this morning about the article on today's front page. To say the least, I wasn't pleased." His voice filled with regret. "She seemed eager to revisit the crime scene to poke around so I ordered her to stay away from the castle."

And in that instant, all those scattered pieces of evidence – from the past and present – formed into a barely visible path, one full of bent limbs, crushed ferns, and muddy indentations, yet still managing to point in a clear direction.

"I'm not saying I know a lot about women, Ben," Hollis began, "but ordering a woman *not* to do something never really pans out."

Ben agreed. "I know exactly where Opal Schatz is."

He fidgeted with his wallet then took off running toward Henry, his arms waving over his head and a $100 bill tucked between his metal fingertips.

CHAPTER 62

No sooner did Henry snatch the cash out of Ben's hand and sit his repeat customer behind him on his blue Jet Ski, than he used his foot to push away from the dock's bumper rail and roar its engine to life.

After a sudden lurching motion, Ben, who had told Henry to *step on it*, had to wrap his arms around Henry's waist to avoid falling off. Ben was glad, if not grateful, Henry made short work of the quarter-mile trip.

Henry pulled up close next to Quill Castle's empty dock, tethering the floating craft while Ben pulled himself onto the dock.

When Ben turned back to thank the teen, he saw Henry distracted, glancing to the left and right sides of Starr Island.

"What?" Ben said.

"Maybe they already left."

"Who?"

"Mrs. Schatz and Mrs. Kennedy. I gave them a hand untying the pontoon boat's mooring line back at the marina. Mrs. Schatz said they were coming out here but I don't see her boat."

Ben's stomach sank. He turned and took off running to the castle. Once inside, he shouted Opal's name on every floor, up every staircase, down every hallway, demanding she answer him.

Silence.

It wasn't until he rounded the corner of the gift shop that he smelled the gunpowder. He drew his gun and crossed the room to examine blood drops near the collapsed floorboards that once cradled the bodies of two teens.

"No. No," Ben cried. He pulled a thin cylinder from his pocket and clicked it on. He waved the flashlight on the debris below until it rested on Opal's bloodied, unconscious face. He scanned the light over her body but could not tell if she was breathing.

"She just fainted. She's not dead," he told himself. He sent a text to Hollis.

I need to get down there.

Ben grabbed the quilt and pillows in the corner and threw them down the shaft. He found the end of nylon rope left behind by Grizzly Adams crew and fed it through the opening between the door and its frame, tying a stopper knot large enough to give him the anchor he needed. With the rope, he formed two large loops on the floor, stepping into the center of each circle and pulling the harness up around his legs. He then sat on the edge of the broken floorboards and yanked on the rope to confirm its strength. He put his pencil flashlight into his mouth before lowering himself into the darkness. With the deftness and confidence of an experienced agent, he rappelled downward into the dark shaft toward the woman he now knew he loved.

In the limited light, Ben had little choice but to lower himself slowly; he maneuvered around wooden debris, ignoring a sharp crack from a beam that didn't like his added weight. When his feet touched the ground adjacent to Opal's crumpled body, he propped the flashlight beside her to assess her injuries. He held his breath when he set his index finger on her bloodied neck, praying to feel her heartbeat under his fingertips.

"That's my girl," he said, a wave of relief rushing through him. He winced at the extent of the injuries to her ankle, face and shoulder. Wanting to prevent shock, Ben covered her with the blanket and gently shimmied the pillow beside her head. He wedged himself into a small, narrow space next to her. When the flashlight rolled off the beam, plunging them into darkness, he didn't move.

"They'll be here in a minute, love. Just hold on a little longer," Ben whispered in her ear. "I'm not going anywhere."

CHAPTER 63

"Can you summarize her injuries?" the medic called down.

"Gunshot wound in her right shoulder, deep facial lacerations, compound fracture of left ankle. She might be going into shock," Ben said. "There's no way to move her."

The rescue team had jumped into action after receiving Hollis Walker's call about a woman trapped in Quill Castle. They lowered a wire basket of items to help Ben – a battery-operated lantern, oxygen cylinder with tubing and mask, bottled water, a spool of gauze.

Ben reached for the lantern first. He flicked it on and hung it on a loose nail, now able to fully grasp their grim reality. "Christ!" he said, loud enough for the rescue team to hear.

Voices murmured above.

"Start with the oxygen tank and tubing," the medic called down. "Do you know how to attach it to the mask?"

"Yes," Ben responded, knowing from the pedantic sound of her voice what she was doing – building his confidence by asking him simple questions. He had used the same tactic whenever a civilian needed to complete a list of activities to ensure escape and survival.

With the mask securely over Opal's mouth and nose, he turned the cylinder valve to release oxygen into Opal's lungs. After a few minutes, he watched Opal's eyes move randomly from side to side before fluttering open.

"Opal," he said. "We'll get you out of here soon. Stay with me."

"Everything hurts," Opal moaned.

Ben looked up to the faces looking down at him. "What's the plan, guys?"

He heard more muffled conversations.

They don't know what to do. There is no plan.

A sudden crack from above transformed those soft murmurs into urgent shouts.

Ben heard a familiar voice call down orders. "The wall is collapsing! Take cover!"

He had only enough time to put his hands over Opal's face before decaying slabs of wooden beams fell around them. Jolts of searing pain erupted in his shoulder.

"Ugh," Ben yelled, coughing hard from the new dust and grime that had forced its way into his lungs. It wasn't until after his spasmodic attempts to find air stopped that he realized he was unable to move his right arm.

"You okay down there?"

"The situation has gone from bad to worse," he called out.

After the dust settled, Ben could see the reason he couldn't move his arm. The end of a newly fallen beam had wedged itself into a corner, pinning his shoulder against the wall. His immovable shoulder had also locked his arm in place, fixing his hand in a levitating position over Opal's face.

It was then he saw the miracle: a rusted spike from a broken beam had been on a direct course to split Opal's face in two when it lodged itself in Ben's titanium hand, its rusted tip now hovering just an inch above her forehead.

Ignoring the biting pain in his shoulder, Ben used his legs to push the rogue beam to its side, extracting the spike from his mechanical hand. He then used his teeth to unscrew the water bottle's cap and spit it to the side. He held the bottle to Opal's lips, grateful that she welcomed the water by swallowing small sips.

The voices above continued their mutterings. While Ben couldn't discern full sentences, he recognized words like *unstable*, *impossible*, and *risky*.

He tilted his chin upwards and called out, "Grizzly Adams!"

"What the hell are you talking about?" called down a voice he knew well.

"Agent Baxter," Ben said, grinning. He was surprised her voice brought him relief.

"Good. You remember me," she quipped. "Who the hell is Grizzly Adams?"

Ben grinned. "Find Hollis. He knows. Grizzly told us that the Singer Castle had hidden exterior entrances for transporting cargo. He thought this castle might have one, too."

"We're on it," she said. "But I need you to listen to me."

Ben watched Opal drift in and out of consciousness.

"Listen up, Agent Franklin. You have probably figured out by now that we can't get her out by bringing her up," Baxter said. "While we look for possible exterior entrances, they are prepared to start jackhammering a hole to extricate her through the limestone foundation."

Ben tried to object but Baxter interrupted.

"So, listen. It might get loud down there. Talk to her. Tell her stories about your career. That will surely bore her to sleep." Baxter hesitated. "Keep her calm, Ben."

Ben nodded. "I can do that."

"And understand. When they have the chance to get Opal out, they are going to take it."

"Yes." He understood if they had the chance to reach in and drag her out by her smashed ankle, they were going to do it. He understood that if the structural integrity of the column was compromised any further, the turret could collapse and kill them both. He understood that Opal's safety was ranked higher than his – the victim's life came first.

"We'll see you both shortly. Baxter out."

Another voice called down a warning. "They're starting now."

A loud rumbling began on the outside east wall, jolting Opal awake. She looked wildly from side to side, then howled in pain. "Where am I? Daniel, what's happening?"

Ben kept his voice low. "We're in Quill Castle. It's Ben. They are trying to get us out."

"I can't breathe," Opal gasped. "I can't breathe." She pushed the mask off her face.

Ben watched her hysteria grow as her eyes darted around, busily calculating the small size of their enclosure. If his shoulder wasn't pinned to the wall, he would have been able to reposition the oxygen mask but he didn't have that luxury.

Not hysteria. Claustrophobia.

Ben grabbed the roll of gauze and tried holding it over her eyes, but Opal wouldn't keep her head still. "I can't breathe," she panted.

Ben knew he needed to remove her awareness of their close quarters, but he couldn't cover her eyes. The answer was right in front of him. He reached up and shut off the lantern. The darkness immediately removed all confining barriers.

"Just listen to my voice. I'm going to tell you a story." He felt Opal's muscles relax.

Ben tilted his head toward her ear, and, amid the growing rumbles outside, told Opal a story that mattered to him more than any other.

CHAPTER 64

"I like birds," he began softly. "When I was a kid I would accompany my mom to her Tuesday-Thursday Biology lecture classes at Fredonia State. That's about three hours southwest of here," he said, "in a town about the size of a hiccup."

Opal kept her head rested into the crux of his free arm.

Ben continued his story. "My mom, Dr. Stephanie Franklin, specialized in ornithology, and my job was to serve as her assistant by clicking the slide machine button to scroll through photos of different bird species for a sleepy undergraduate audience. My favorite day each semester was the day Mom mimicked the calls of common New York State birds. You should have seen those hungover students jolt awake when she unleashed her high-pitched screech of a red-tailed hawk, or the melodious, rising and falling notes of the rose-breasted grosbeak, or the woo-hoo of the black and white chickadee, or the sharp, redundant, squeal of the common sparrow."

Rumbling motors fell silent. Ben saw Opal's eyes open, her vacant stare resting on the wall.

Baxter called down. "The Canadian Coast Guard just pulled over Bree as she crossed into their territory upriver. They said they saw her throw something into the water, maybe some type of fabric. Any idea what that could have been?"

Ben disregarded her question. "She can't communicate right now, Baxter," he said, but Opal started to moan.

"I'm right here. Do you know what she's talking about?"

She nodded slightly and spoke softly. "We were looking for a ribbon with Enzo's and Ellie's blood on it. That would have sealed Enzo's guilt. We found a bloody apron instead. It was the only thing linking Enzo to attacking Ellie." She whimpered in exhaustion.

Ben called up her description of events.

"Shit," Baxter said.

A few thuds from their rescuers on an outside wall made Opal flinch and moan in pain before falling silent. Her breaths deepened.

Baxter called down. "Keep an eye out on the east wall for a latch or handle. It's going to get loud down there."

When Ben flicked on the lantern, he was relieved to see Opal's eyes closed. Was she asleep? Unconscious? He only knew he needed her alive.

Whether she heard him or not, Ben kept his voice low and easy. "You know, sparrows are real pains in the ass. They never shut up and build their nests out of garbage." He pointed his mangled metallic finger to a nest built on a rafter. "The one across from us has a wire twist-tie woven into it; the one up there has Styrofoam packing peanuts sticking out in all directions."

He looked up at the sides of the worn wooden walls of the column and noticed abandoned bird nests lining the walls all the way up to the turret.

"I wish you could see this," he said. "Luke Annetti had told me that most of the turrets had collapsed by the sixties, allowing birds and bats to fly in and out at will until repairs were made in the seventies."

A weak hum escaped Opal's lips.

It was then that a red flicker caught Ben's eye. At the bottom of the lowest sparrow nest, the one right across from him, he saw a flash of red on white. He reached out his mangled hand and, after a few attempts, used a sharp wire sticking out from his knuckle to hook a thin strip of frayed fabric. Gently, he pulled out a worn, white ribbon stained with maroon blotches.

"Would you look at that?" he said.

Agent Baxter interrupted his find. "They found some kind of access door at the castle's base. They're going to use a crowbar to pry it open to your immediate right. Cover yourselves."

"All set!" Ben secured the ribbon to his chest, then grabbed the quilt and pulled it over their heads.

Within moments, loud booms and rusty squeals began outside, ending in a loud pop. He lifted the blanket and saw an unexpected sight – sunlight.

"Hey there, Agent Franklin."

"Baxter," Ben said. "I need an evidence bag." He held out the tattered, stained ribbon. "You'll find that this has the blood of Ellie McAllister and Enzo Kennedy."

"Good to see you, too," she said. Baxter pushed in her hand holding the clear baggie and watched Ben drop in the ribbon. "I'll deliver it myself. Look, the medics have a good plan and are ready to get both of you out. But I should tell you one last thing," she said.

"What's that?" Ben asked.

"Your retirement has been accepted," she said. "Effective immediately."

CHAPTER 65

Two days later, Ruby sat in a hospital room visitor chair holding her unconscious mother's hand, careful not to disturb her IV tubing. Doctors told her that Opal should start to wake within the hour.

On Ruby's lap, under a pile of crumpled tissues, lay a pink piece of copy paper sealed in a clear baggie. The FBI sticker in the center didn't prevent Ruby from reading and rereading Howard's attempt at an explanation.

~~Ruby, I know you might hate me, but I will always love you.~~
~~I'm sorry to have to tell you this, but...~~
~~I betrayed my brother. He never knew I loved your mother. We were together for just one night. I found out when she came back with Daniel and you. One look at your eyes and I knew.~~
~~Funny story, I'm not just you're uncle...~~
~~I understand if you never forgive me.~~
~~In time, maybe you can understand why we kept it a secret.~~

More than anything, Ruby wanted two things from her mother – to hold her close and to push her far away. Over the last two days, Ruby received regular updates during Opal's seventeen hours of surgery while skilled hands reconstructed her shattered ankle and replaced a crushed hip. Ruby hadn't left her side since being moved into her private room.

Jin poked his head inside the curtain. "I got the test results from the obstetrician. Your baby is healthy."

Ruby covered her face and sobbed into her hands. Jin knelt and wrapped Ruby in his arms, her sobs dampening his shoulder. "You vomited most of the poison at the scene, keeping a lethal dose out of your bloodstream. Your baby is healthy," he repeated.

Ruby felt him pull away. When she opened her eyes, she saw that Hyo had replaced her father kneeling at her feet.

"I have a few things to say," Hyo said.

Ruby nodded, bracing herself for more heartache.

Hyo gripped her hands. "I am highly skilled in the art of medicine, but you are naturally skilled in the art of life. You have the uncanny ability to accept what you can't control and deal with it. I don't, and I can't promise I will ever learn how to do that. I can only offer you my flawed, over-thinking, egotistical self who will regularly fall below your reasonable level of expectation." Hyo slid a small silver trinket box into her hands.

Ruby slid off her chair to the floor beside Hyo and opened the box. A thin platinum band ring with three round diamonds. "It's beautiful."

"It was my grandmother's," Hyo said.

Ruby wiggled the ring out of the box and slid it over the tip of her finger, before withdrawing it. She looked at Hyo. "We have to talk about the baby."

"No. We have to talk about *our* baby," Hyo corrected.

Ruby shook her head. "I want to be over-the-moon excited right now, but I can't allow myself to get lost in this moment. The bottom line is that the people I love most, the ones I hold most dear, betrayed me. They kept secrets."

Hyo pulled back. "So did you."

Ruby pulled back. "Are you kidding me right now?"

"Why did you keep the fact that you wanted to be a mother secret from me?"

"That's not the same thing," Ruby said. "It's a completely different situation."

"Answer the question," Hyo insisted. "Why did you keep the fact that you wanted to be a mother secret from me?"

Ruby thought to herself. She whispered, "I thought you might leave me."

"Could Opal and Howard have thought that, too? Could they have thought they could have lost you by telling you the truth?"

Ruby looked to the ceiling, managing only a nod.

"I can't offer you perfection," Hyo said. "But I know one thing for sure: even with the obvious unknowns, we will forge ahead on this uncharted path, together."

Ruby fiddled with the ring and slid it onto her finger and planted a soft kiss on Hyo's lips.

A moan from Opal moved the women to their feet. Hyo checked her vitals while Ruby leaned in close to her mother's face.

"Mom," Ruby said. "I'm here."

Opal opened her eyes and focused them on Ruby for a few seconds before sleep again overtook her.

Hyo was pleased with the numbers. "Dad said she would wake up in about an hour."

"I'll call Ben," Ruby said, who grabbed her purse and walked toward the door. "He'll want to be here."

"Wait," Hyo said. "Anyone else you should include?"

Ruby's eyes glanced at the pink paper on the chair, but she turned and left.

CHAPTER 66

Seventy-two hours after the EMTs pulled Opal and Ben out of Quill Castle through an iron access door, Opal sat in her hospital bed, propped up behind a tray of cherry gelatin containers and plastic water cups with straws. Her most prominent square bandages covered her cheek and shoulder, while a solid cast secured the bones in her ankle. Purple and gray skin contusions were visible in places her cotton gown didn't cover.

She looked around at her room stuffed with visitors. Ruby sat at her side, with both Dr. Byongs standing behind her. Ben stood at her other side by the window, fiddling with the planters to make sure the hostas didn't get pushed to the floor by the vases of roses and carnations. Howard was the last to arrive, nodding sheepishly to Ruby and choosing to remain in the doorway.

"Is this an intervention?" Opal quipped.

Ben took that as his cue to begin. "I have a great deal of information to share as we wrap up our investigation, but there are some gaping holes I'm hoping some of you might be able to fill." He turned to Opal, touched her forehead and stroked her hair to the side. "If you get too tired, just say so. We can always do this tomorrow."

Opal glanced at Ruby, who shot back a *he is being totally adorable* look at her mother. Opal could only roll her eyes before turning back to Ben and nodding for him to begin.

"Enzo Kennedy has been formally charged with the June 1990 rape of Ellie McAllister at Quill Castle. She kept the attack a secret because she believed she was protecting her husband and their future. Ellie was released last night from the psych facility and into Mac's care. Mac is angry at Ellie for not telling him, angry at Enzo for lying to him, and angry at himself for not demanding the truth from Ellie decades ago. They would both benefit from your friendship as they recover.

He continued. "Enzo is now under investigation for the assault or rape of sixteen women over the last forty years. During his initial questioning, he insisted he was innocent until I held up the white ribbon stained with blood."

Opal hummed in satisfaction.

"At that point, Enzo said he would never provide a new DNA sample to match the blood on the ribbon. What he didn't know was that we already had a fresh sample. After Ellie had scratched him so deeply during the interrogation, I had our forensics team scrape Ellie's fingernails for skin and blood samples. From that data, we expect the number of victims to double when his DNA is entered into the FBI's system. When this goes public tomorrow, our profilers say the numbers could triple. By the end of the week, we will have a better understanding of the geographical scope of his assaults."

"You can raise that number to seventeen right now," Hyo said.

"No," Jin cried out.

Hyo squeezed her father's hand, nodding that she needed to tell her story. "When I was a junior in high school, I started taking painting lessons from Mrs. Kennedy at their house. I only ever went there for one day. It was the day after I got my driver's license. I remember how excited I was to tell Mrs. Kennedy about it." Hyo took a deep breath and exhaled. "At the end of the watercolor lesson, Mrs. Kennedy left the room to wash brushes in the kitchen sink, and, in seconds, that bastard was on me with one hand down my shorts and the other up my shirt. He didn't expect me to kick him in the balls so hard that he would fall to his knees and squeal like the pig he was."

"You were a minor when this happened," Ben said.

"Seventeen."

Ben jotted that down. "I'll set you up first thing in the morning to give your statement to Agent Ameth Baxter at police headquarters."

Hyo nodded. Jin wiped away tears. Hyo hugged him close, offering assurances. "Dad. Look at me today. He didn't destroy me. It was Mrs. Kennedy who destroyed my hope in humanity."

Ben frowned. "What role, did Bree Kennedy play in the assault?"

Hyo struggled with her words. "After I kicked him, Mrs. Kennedy rushed back into the room and saw Enzo writhing in pain. She looked at each of us and did nothing. She said nothing. She just put the brushes back on the easel, smiled, and told me that the art lessons needed to end, that she was no longer available for private lessons. She made it seem like it was my fault, but she knew. She knew what he did to me and did nothing."

Ruby saw Opal shudder. "We should stop. You need to rest."

"No," Opal said. "This needs to be over once and for all." She nodded at Ben. "How did you find us at Quinn Castle?"

"Henry."

"As in Mitch's Henry?" Opal said.

Ben nodded. "At the dock, he told me that he saw you and Bree board the *My Gem IV* in the marina. I texted Hollis to find your boat on the river while I found you at the castle."

Ben looked at Howard, who took a step forward. "I just wanted to say I'm sorry for any pain and suffering my wife has caused any of you."

"Howard," Ben said. "Please accept my condolences. Is it okay with you if I discuss the details surrounding her case?"

Howard nodded.

"Bree Kennedy has been charged with the first-degree murder of Claudine Schatz," he said. "Investigators found a photo of Enzo's hand injury from his hospital file on Claudine's phone. Our profilers say that there's a chance she might have been a victim of Enzo's in the past, but we haven't been able to confirm that. We are working with the theory that Bree was trying to protect Enzo."

Opal interjected softly. "Just like Ellie."

Ben continued. "We served search warrants for both Manor Oak and the Schatz home. Our labs confirmed that the peach pie and jar of peaches found in Howard's office both contained high levels of arsenic, a box of which was found in Claudine's kitchen. Because the victims were poisoned with *peaches* laced with arsenic, we are exhuming Daniel Schatz's body to run additional toxicology tests," he said.

It was Ruby's turn to ask questions to Howard. "How could she have done this to my father, to us?"

Howard shifted his weight against the doorway. "Claudine wasn't a happy woman. She told me once that discovering the dagger at the estate sale was a sign she was destined for greater things in life than baking peach pies. When Daniel's student's essay ran in the newspaper and that curator from New York came forward, Claudine became unhinged, thinking my brother had a personal vendetta against her. The more I tried to tell her she was wrong about him, the more determined, the more certain she became. After Daniel died, she apologized to me for being so hateful, but I never suspected that my wife would have the capability of murdering my brother, the man I betrayed."

Ben returned to the conversation, not noticing Opal's frown. "Howard, I am the one responsible for sharing your private letter with Ruby. When my team revisited the scene, they had bagged the letter from your desk. When the letter's context was revealed to me, I had three choices: I could let the letter be transcribed into evidence to eventually become public record, return it to its owner who was unconscious in ICU, or deliver it to the intended recipient." Ben said. "I needed to make the call, so I chose the last choice, the one that gave you the most privacy."

Howard and Opal shared a glance.

Howard focused back on Ruby. "Then you know."

Ruby nodded. "I know that you're my biological father, yes."

"I'm sorry, Ruby," Opal said. "I should have told you." The machines attached to Opal started beeping; a red warning light flashed above the heart monitor screen.

"It's not her fault," Howard said, stepping forward. "Blame me."

"Both of you stop," Ruby said, glancing first at her mother and then at Howard.

Opal put her head back on her pillow and took several deep breaths, relaxing the technology hooked to her heart.

Ruby stepped to the end of Opal's bed. "I see your secret for what it was – a miracle. The baby will now grow up with a grandmother and grandfather. So, both of you look at me," she demanded. They obliged. "I forgive you. Both of you. I am living proof that your lie did more *good* than harm."

She held her hand out to Hyo, who grabbed it with both hands.

Howard put his hand over his chest in consolation and relief.

But Opal frowned again. "It must be the anesthetic talking, but I'm still unclear about one thing."

"What's that?" Ruby asked.

"What baby?"

For the rest of the afternoon, sunshine streamed through the hospital window as Opal's attention darted in different directions. She listened attentively to Ruby's stories about her visits to the Syracuse fertility clinic, assured Hyo that she would be a marvelous parent, and laughed as Howard told Ruby about the time Daniel got his head stuck in the ball return at Lucky Lanes when they were kids.

Listening to his story confirmed what Opal realized was now true, that Howard would be able to keep Daniel in their lives in a way she never could.

"Everyone out," a nurse barked. "Even you two," she said, pointing to Hyo and Jin. "The patient needs to rest." Each person followed the order after squeezing Opal's hand and pecking her on the cheek with a quick kiss. She welcomed the deep sleep that quickly found her.

CHAPTER 67

A repetitive, deep noise coaxed Opal awake. She found the darkness outside confusing until she looked at the wall clock. Hours had passed; the head nurse must have let her sleep through dinner. The source of the sound, louder than before, was at her side.

She was surprised to see an old man asleep in the chair next to her; he wore a crumpled, tweed suit and matching hat, one that had slipped forward over his face. He sawed log after log. She wished she could extend her arm far enough to him to tap his shoulder, but tubes and monitors limited her mobility.

"Mr. Burton?" Opal said. Ash didn't stir. She cleared her throat and yelled his name loudly. "Mr. Burton!"

Ash Burton sprung awake and quickly adjusted his hat back onto his head. He looked at Opal and grinned. "I'm sorry to disturb you. I heard about what happened and, to be honest, you look even worse than I had expected."

"Thanks a lot," she said.

"But I need you to know something straight away. It's about Faith Quill."

"*Seriously*," Opal thought. She kept her voice polite, yet direct. "I'm pretty banged up right now. The last people I'm thinking about are the Quills."

Ignoring her hint, he leaned forward and set a thin stack of cardstock papers on her lap.

"What are these?" she asked.

"Event menus the Quills used for their formal dinners. Look what's on the back."

Opal narrowed her eyes at Ash, then flipped over the first menu. When she read the secret note on the back, Opal's eyes opened wide. She continued through the stack, flipping each one over to read the private correspondence that no one, outside of the two lovers, was ever supposed to read.

Opal looked at Ash. "It's proof. Faith Quill *was* having an affair," Opal said. She thumbed through the stack. "One message was marked with an E at the end. Do you know who she was writing to?"

Ash scratched his head. "I was hoping you could fill in that blank. In your research, have you ever come across the last name Mosley?"

Opal thought hard, but her eyebrows sank. She handed the stack of menus back to Ash. "I don't think so. Have you?"

Ash nodded and leaned in. "Twice, actually. In an old ledger, Everett Mosley's name appeared in Griffin Quill's payroll records until October 17, 1902. That's just a few days after he wrote the last note to her on the menu saying he was leaving."

Opal suddenly felt like a memory was clawing its way into her narcotic-infused brain. She needed more details to trigger a breakthrough. "When else?"

"Yesterday. A Manor Oak nurse, Rosa, who once took care of my Vivian, delivered this to me." Ash held up a faded envelope marked with a black-inked, frilly Q in the center. "She said her patient, Xavier Everett Mosley, asked her to give two photos and a letter to an heir of the Quill family. She said he didn't just ask her; he had begged her."

"My Everett," Opal whispered, forcing her anesthetic haze to lift. "When I was at the castle, I found a photograph of Faith Quill holding hands with her servant. 'My Everett' was written on the back."

He slid a scalloped-edged, black-and-white photograph from the envelope and handed it to her. "This photo?"

She took it from him, examining it closely. There they were – Griffin and Faith – dressed in their Sunday best at the Alex Bay Carnival. She again saw Faith's hand intertwined with the servant who stood behind her. "That's it." She flipped it over, but it was blank.

Ash's spunk returned. His eyes glistened in the fluorescent lights.

Her interest piqued, Opal struggled to prop herself up a bit straighter in bed. "Who was in the other photo?"

Ash handed it to her.

She ran her fingertips over the colorful image and inspected it closely, seeing nothing familiar. "A family swimming in the ocean."

Opal looked at Ash, perplexed. She turned it over and saw '1970, Montauk' written in pencil.

Ash pointed. "Look at the man lying on the blue floaty with the child, the one across from the kids on the innertubes. Look at the birthmark on his back."

When Opal saw the elongated white blotches across the man's brown back, she instinctively raised the palm of her hand to the bandages covering her maroon-stained cheek. Like a movie reel casting a documentary on a screen, she flashed through decades of appointments in physicians' offices, for herself and for Ruby, listening to the technical and genetic differences between birthmarks and auto-immune skin pigment diseases; Opal knew the name of the man's condition.

Opal tapped the photo. "No. Those aren't birthmarks like mine and Ruby's. That's vitiligo, not port wine. He might not have had the faded pigment areas at birth like Ruby and me."

Ash nodded. His voice was soft and genuine. "Both are beautiful."

Opal's eyes welled with tears. "You have a good heart, Mr. Burton. Thank you for looking beyond the surface, for finding what was within." Opal moved her hand to her heart.

Ash nodded again.

When she felt her tears sting the stitches under the gauze, Opal shifted the conversation back to the reason for Ash's visit. She cleared her throat. "But there's no way the man in this photo could be my Everett; that man looks about twenty years old."

Then Ash said the sentence that filled in his own blank. "But Xavier Mosley *would* fit a timeline of being Everett Mosley's grandson."

Opal let Ash's words sink in before connecting the dots. "And if Everett and Faith are Pearl's biological parents, that would make Everett my great-grandfather, not Griffin Quill." She locked eyes with Ash and read his troubled face and frowned. "What aren't you telling me?"

Ash's shoulders drooped; his eyebrows creased in concern. "Rosa called to give me the news. Xavier Everett Mosley died early this morning."

Surprising them both, sudden sobs escaped Opal's throat, the poignant and gut-wrenching news overwhelming her emotions. "This is unfair! Why did he even come here?" She no longer cared about the stinging tears on her cheek.

Ash scooted his chair closer to Opal's bed. "Rosa said Xavier Mosley came to Alex Bay to apologize to the Quill family for his grandfather being a coward."

Opal blinked twice. "A coward?"

Looking apologetic, Ash gave Opal the envelope. "See for yourself."

Opal opened the yellow-tinted flap and slid out the onion-skin paper, running her finger over the Quill crest at the top center. She skimmed it quickly, noting the identity of the author and the letter's intended recipient, before reading it again, slowly and thoughtfully.

January 4, 1904

My Everett,

Our Pearl will turn two soon, and my tortured soul sees more of you in her dark eyes and her graceful silhouette with each passing day. Without you near, I grow weaker, as though a leech drains my will to live. A part of you should take solace in knowing that Griffin loves Pearl as he loves Griffin, Jr., and Cecelia. I assure you he has never had a doubt.

Griffin has shipped me off to Manhattan where expert physicians from France, from Belgium, from London, poke and prod at me day and night, searching for the source of my deteriorating muscles and weakening lungs. I want to tell them the cause, that there is no cure for heartache, that there is no cure for heartbreak. Only you can save me.

Come back to me. Come back to me. Please, my Everett. Come back to me.

All my love,
Your Faith

Opal looked at Ash. "It's a love letter from Faith to Everett written three days before she died." She rubbed her forehead. "But what does this have to do with Xavier seeing himself as a coward?"

"Not Xavier. Everett." Ash said. "Everett Mosley never answered Faith's letter. He never went to her. Rosa said Xavier was trying to end a curse under which his family had never been able to escape. Xavier decided to act. After receiving a grim diagnosis from his doctor, he had arranged to transfer to Alexandria Bay for the last months of his life." Ash wiped his eyes. "He wanted you to know how his grandfather had suffered, how much he had regretted his decision to abandon Faith."

Opal whispered to Ash. "Faith Quill did die of a broken heart after all."

Ash nodded. "It's like you said: history is often more complex than it seems." He tipped his hat at her.

Opal rested her head on her pillow. Before she spoke, she exhaled a long, soothing breath. "Adding the Mosley names to the system would probably unlock the rest of Pearl's hereditary line." She whispered to him. "He could be the missing link to fulfill the rest of the Birthstone Branch."

Opal shifted her hand toward Ash, who reached out and gently held it in his. Their glazed eyes shared a smile and nod at the discovery of a hidden love that led to Opal's very existence.

"Thank you for sharing this with me." Opal tucked the photos and letter back into the envelope and slid it toward Ash.

He hesitated. "You don't want to make copies of those?"

She shook her head. "They had meant for those thoughts to be private, so let's keep it that way."

Ash took the envelope, added it to the stack of menus in his hand, and stood. "I will keep them safe."

"I have no doubt," Opal said. "Thank you, Mr. Burton."

He tipped his hat to her, then turned and left, enjoying a jovial spring in each step.

"Don't you ever stop working?" Roxie asked. She was decked out in her black Toronto Raptors jersey with a basketball tucked under her elbow and a gym bag slung off her shoulder.

"Oh, thank God," Opal said wearily. "You have to break me out of here."

Roxie evaluated her injuries from head to toe. "Shattered ankle, stitched-up head, broken hip. You are stuck here, sista."

"How are the two of you holding things down at the paper?"

"Three of us. Our newest reporter has been doing a bang-up job."

"You hired someone?" Opal said.

"He had quite the sob story. Something about needing to pay his car insurance after saving the life of his dad's boss."

"Henry," Opal said.

"So, look. I didn't bring you any flowers. I brought you something better." Roxie raised her eyebrows with anticipation when she plopped the newest issue of AARP's monthly magazine on the hospital bed.

Opal moaned. She picked up the magazine and looked at herself on its front cover. There she was, leaning against a stone wall of Quill Castle with a headline that stated how it all began.

Small Town Editor Writes Gem of a Story

"Since you're famous now, it probably wouldn't be a bad time to give your star employee another raise," Roxie said.

"I can't be responsible for anything I agreed to while under the influence of a narcotic."

Roxie then spoke in a tone she rarely used. "I was scared I had lost you. I listened to the scanner when they brought you out. You were in bad shape."

Opal grabbed her hand. "And I'm okay now. I'll be back soon."

"We'll see."

"What does that mean?"

"Ebony White stopped by the office this morning," Roxie said. She nodded to the magazine. "She brought that preview issue with her, along with lots and lots of ideas for follow-up projects and books and documentaries. You're about to move up in the world."

"I'm not going anywhere. You, by the way, are currently the lead reporter for the biggest crime story east of the Mississippi, so, in my book, you've already moved up in the world."

"I got Ebony checked into the Bijou House. We're going to do shots later."

"On the court?"

She blinked. "In a bar."

"Maybe she'll offer you a book deal, too," Opal said.

"Looks like those narcotics are indeed working," Roxie said. "But I wanted you to know something else. I covered Claudine's funeral today. Lots of guests. Lots of press."

"Did you interview Howard?"

"Briefly. He said Claudine was a woman with strong convictions." They shared a knowing glance. "When I wrote the article, I didn't mention that she might get a posthumous murder conviction for Daniel's death. I'll wait for the weekend edition for that." She winked.

Opal rubbed her eyes. "Absolutely no part of me has come to terms with Claudine's diabolical mind. My sister-in-law likely premeditated the poisoning and murder of my husband over a dagger she somehow thought defined her. And then she planned on wiping out Ruby and me, and almost Howard, over a past that was never hers to begin with."

"You have some pretty fucked up friends," Roxie said.

Opal smiled. "One of my high school teachers used to call the four of us the Quirky Quadruplets, but The Four Fibbers would have been more accurate."

"Those are the drugs talking. Come on. Get some rest."

Opal looked slyly at Roxie. "Seeing Hollis tonight?"

Roxie smirked. "You know about that?"

"Like yesterday's news."

MARCH 17, 2016

"That is ridiculous," Ben said.

"It is not," Opal insisted. "I had a very nice uncle with that name."

"I assure you that they are not naming their child Wilbur," Ben said, snapping closed his copy of *Thirty Thousand Baby Names*. They would be dooming him to be called "Some Pig" for the rest of his life," he said. "And don't you dare suggest Wilhelmina for a girl."

They sat snuggled beside each other on a couch in Opal's glassed-in Florida room watching another inch of New York lake-effect snow climb its way up the glass window. Her backyard gardens and branches were buried under heavy white pillows. Opal's cane rested on the end table that held their steaming mugs of coffee, appropriately spiked with Irish whisky. They watched flames dance in the fireplace, only to be distracted by a cardinal landing on a dormant apple tree limb, its red-on-white contrast brought Opal a moment of needed peace.

Ben leaned over and kissed Opal on the cheek. "What do you think the baby will call you? There are lots of choices now: Grandma, Granny, Gammy, Gigi, Gaga, Mimi and Grandmama."

"Good God, tell me you are joking," she said.

She swiftly returned her attention to her own baby-name book, browsing the lists of seemingly endless options. Opal gasped. "Guess what the name Kennedy means?"

"What?" Ben said.

"Unlucky."

"That's an understatement in about a hundred different ways."

Ben reopened his copy and turned to the S section. "I have a fast fact of my own. The name Schatz, which is a popular name for German males, happens to mean pearl. So, your name technically means…"

"Opal Pearl. How fitting," she said, flitting her eyelashes at him. She leaned forward and grabbed the silver jewelry box off the coffee table.

"Have you made a decision yet?" Ben asked.

She shook her head and pried it open. For about the hundredth time, she lifted the pearl necklace and ruby bracelet from the box, admiring them in awe. "I'm still stunned Hollis gave them to me."

"The court determined that Xavier Mosely was operating with a sound mind and body when he spoke to his nurse. The jewels Ellie had slipped into her pocket the night of the accident are rightfully yours," Ben said, before adding a sarcastic flair to his voice. "That is, until word spreads and other relatives come out of the woodwork and stop by one day just to say hello."

Opal smirked, dismissing his suggestion.

"These will make grand Christmas gifts for Ruby and Hyo." She closed the box, noticing Ben staring blankly at his phone. "He hasn't returned any of your calls?"

"Not a one, and Rico has strongly advised me not to visit or contact Luke Annetti," Ben said. "I'm told he will never accept that his son's death was an accident, that he wants Ellie prosecuted to the fullest extent of the law."

"I can relate. Even though Claudine is dead, there is still a sliver of me that wants her alive so I can watch her rot in hell. What does that make me?"

"Human," Ben said. He reached his arms around Opal, pulling her close.

Opal looked into the eyes of the man beside her, the man who had saved her in more ways than one. "What do you think is the meaning of a gray-haired, metal-handed man falling for an older, scarred, permanently limping woman?"

"Lucky," Ben said.

The sudden vibrations from Opal's phone interrupted the moment. In one swift swipe, she accepted the call. She listened, smiled, and touched her fingers to her cheek.

"Congratulations, Hyo. Wonderful news. Yes, I will tell him. Kiss my daughter for me," she said, ending the call.

"Well?" Ben said. "Will the birthstone branch continue or end?"

She snuggled into the crux of Ben's shoulder. "From Pearl to Jade to Opal to Ruby to a new, little jewel. We have ourselves an Emmy."

Catherine D'Agostino

CLAUDINE'S PEACH PIE RECIPE

Serves many.

Ingredients

6-8 peaches, preferably ripe

1/3 cup granulated sugar

1/4 cup brown sugar

1/3 cup flour

1/2 teaspoon ground cinnamon

1/4 teaspoon nutmeg

1/4 teaspoon salt

1 1/2 tablespoons lemon juice

1/2 teaspoon vanilla extract

1 egg yolk

2 tablespoons of water

Add *nothing* else.

Instructions
1. After preparing two crusts, use the first crust to line a pie pan, then preheat oven to 400 degrees.
2. Blanch 6-8 large peaches. Drain, peel and slice peaches into a large bowl.
3. On top of the peaches, add both sugars, flour, cinnamon, nutmeg, salt, lemon juice, and vanilla extract. Mix thoroughly and gently.
4. Pour peach mixture into crust, then lay the second crust over the pie. Seal the edges.
5. After combining the egg yolk and water in a small dish, brush the mixture on the crust.
6. Make two, inch-long slashes in the top crust to allow steam to escape during baking.

Bake for 45 minutes atop a sheet tray to catch juices that might erupt from within.

DISCUSSION QUESTIONS

1. Opal, Claudine, Ellie and Bree all kept secrets. To what extent does each secret impact her life and the lives of their families? Which of those secrets would also classify as lies?
2. Who are the victims and who are the victimized?
3. How are Ellie and Bree similar?
4. Choose adjectives to describe Enzo. Besides Bree, what other characters were unknowingly giving him power?
5. Irony occurs when an actual outcome is the opposite of what readers or characters had expected. List an example of irony regarding Claudine, Howard, Ellie, Bree, Enzo and Ben.
6. Which characters have physical flaws and how do those flaws reflect their identity and their decisions?
7. A quill is an instrument used to write letters. Discuss the impact of the letters and notes written throughout the story?
8. How was Enzo able to prey on women for so long?
9. Which relationships in the novel were healthy and why?
10. Think about Hyo and Ruby's relationship. What fine line between truth and lies almost ends their relationship?
11. Claudine's hubris led to her making mistakes. What other characters made mistakes that changed the course of their future?
12. Early in the novel, Howard reflects that he felt trapped in his marriage. What did he lose and gain by the end of the story?

13. Which specific lies contribute to the book's title?
14. In what way was Agent Ben Franklin's titanium hand more of a personal blessing than a curse?
15. Discuss Ash Burton's character and motivation. What made him tick?
16. Are all lies unacceptable all of the time? Under what conditions, if any, would a lie be appropriate? Should any character have kept a lie a secret?
17. Ellie prayed every day. What thoughts or requests do you think she shared with God?
18. Roxie quoted Doris Lessing when she stated that "Living in a small town anywhere means preserving oneself behind a mask." Later, Hollis states that he thinks people who live in small towns tend to settle disputes using revenge. Based on your knowledge of how small towns function, do you find any truth in their statements? Explain.

In Memoriam

To my John David III
June 7, 2007

Shakespeare was right.
"There *is* a special providence in the fall of a sparrow."
Hamlet

Made in the USA
Middletown, DE
29 August 2023